"She didn't kill Amy!" Heidi blurted

Tears sprang to her eyes. "Dana's family lives next door to mine. We grew up like sisters. I know her as well as I know myself. She's *dying* in that prison, Gideon." Her voice trembled. "I've got to get her out of there or my life's not going to be worth living, either."

"Lord," she heard him whisper.

"When I found out that a famous detective from San Diego's homicide division was teaching a criminology course in my classroom, I considered it a godsend. That's wh—"

"You don't need to explain," he interjected.

"You'll never know how grateful I am that you let me join the class. I've already learned so much. I *know* vital evidence was overlooked in her case." Heidi gazed up at Gideon. "The other night I phoned John Cobb, Dana's attorney."

"He's one of the best around."

She took a deep breath. "I hope you're right, Gideon. He believes in Dana's innocence, but he said that unless we come up with compelling new evidence, he wouldn't be able to get the case reopened."

"That's because he knows how difficult it is."

"But surely it's not impossible...."

He reached out to squeeze her hand. "No. Nothing's impossible if you want it badly enough."

Dear Reader,

Recently I saw a documentary about a retired newspaper reporter who happened to be at a local library doing some genealogy and came across a twenty-year-old article about a murder that had been committed in the town where she lived. Being curious by nature, she made enquiries and found out the case was still open.

Intrigued, she started to dig around, talk to the police, interview people who knew the victim. Within a few months she'd solved the crime. There was a trial and the culprit was imprisoned.

When she was asked how she was able to do what no detective had managed to accomplish, she chuckled before answering. "I don't know why. Perhaps it was a fresh eye, a new look at an old problem—the answer just seemed obvious to me."

By the time the documentary was over, I had plotted *My Private Detective*, a romance novel in which a good cop, Gideon Poletti, brings a fresh eye to a closed murder case—only to fall madly in love with the convicted woman's friend…who might know more than she's telling.

Happy reading!

Rebecca Winters

P.S. If you have access to the Internet, I hope you'll visit my Web site at http://www.rebeccawinters-author.com

My Private Detective
Rebecca Winters

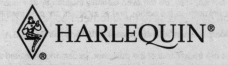

TORONTO • NEW YORK • LONDON
AMSTERDAM • PARIS • SYDNEY • HAMBURG
STOCKHOLM • ATHENS • TOKYO • MILAN • MADRID
PRAGUE • WARSAW • BUDAPEST • AUCKLAND

ISBN 0-373-71005-4

MY PRIVATE DETECTIVE

Visit us at www.eHarlequin.com

Printed in U.S.A.

My Private Detective

CHAPTER ONE

"MR. COBB REALLY TOLD YOU there's nothing more he can do?"

"Yes."

Heidi Ellis felt her heart plunge as she stared at her best friend through the Plexiglas partition at Fielding Women's Prison outside San Bernardino, California.

Dana Turner had always been a tall, dark-haired, vibrant beauty. But seven and a half months of confinement had already taken their toll.

Haunted by the pale, fragile-looking creature, who'd grown even thinner since her last visit, Heidi feared her friend wouldn't last the year in this place, let alone thirty more. She was in prison for the murder of her sister—a murder she didn't commit.

Heidi gripped the phone receiver more tightly. "I don't believe that."

"You have to," Dana said in a dull voice. "He's supposed to be one of the best criminal attorneys in Southern California. I'm resigned to the fact that this is my life from now on."

"I'll *never* be resigned to it!"

"You don't have a choice. I told Mom and Dad the same thing. They're so devastated that every time they see me, they age another year."

That wasn't surprising. They'd lost Amy, and now their older daughter was wrongfully incarcerated for her murder.

"I think it would be better if no one came to visit me anymore. It can only drag everyone down further than they already are."

None of the Ellises—neither Heidi nor her parents— had been subpoenaed to testify at Dana's trial. In fact, Dana had asked that they not attend. It had made Heidi feel so helpless. She still felt that way, but anger had begun to replace her fears.

"You know me better than that, Dana. I refuse to just sit by. There *has* to be a way to reopen your case and get it heard again. Someone else killed your sister. Whoever committed the crime is running around free while you're…"

Her voice trailed off because she was afraid she'd dissolve in tears in front of Dana. That wasn't going to help her friend. Taking a deep breath to compose herself, she said, "I'm not sure how to go about it, but I'm going to find a way to get you out of here, no matter what I have to do!"

Dana's sweet smile tore Heidi's heart to shreds. "I love you for being so loyal. But there's a time to quit, and this is it."

"No! As soon as I leave here, I'm going to call your lawyer and ask him exactly what I have to do in order to get the court to take another look at your case."

Her friend shook her head sadly. "He's worked tirelessly on my behalf. If he says it's all over, then it is."

"He's only one person, Dana. No one's infallible. I'm thinking of hiring someone else and starting from scratch. Dad's attorney knows a trial lawyer in Los Angeles who has the same kind of reputation as Mr. Cobb. If your attorney can't help, then I'm phoning this other attorney as soon as I get home this evening.''

Dana frowned. "Don't you dare use your money to try to help me. You'd be throwing it away. I couldn't bear that.''

"My mom and dad love you, too, Dana. They told me they want to contribute because they believe in your innocence. They've known you all your life!''

Dana's lovely face crumpled, and she broke down sobbing.

"I'm going to get you out of here. As long as you're behind these bars, I'll never be happy again.''

"Don't say that. You've got your own life to live.''

"What life would that be? We're like sisters! When you bleed, so do I. You'd stand by me no matter what, so let's not resume *that* discussion. When you go to sleep tonight, be assured that I've already made phone calls to get the process started.''

"You mustn't ruin your life for me!'' Dana cried, burying her face in her hands.

"That's my decision. In fact, the sooner I leave here, the sooner you'll be freed from this place. So I'll say goodbye for now. The next time you see me, I'll be bringing good news. Hold on, Dana. Just hold on.''

She replaced the receiver and stood up. Dana followed suit. They pressed their hands together against the glass. Her friend's ravaged face was the last thing Heidi saw before she turned sharply away and left the building; the last thing she heard was the horrifying sound of doors locking behind her.

To some degree, Dana had always suffered from claustrophobia. Heidi could just imagine how much worse that condition had become since she'd been here. The prison doctor refused to give her medication for it. That was another injustice that needed to be corrected.

As soon as Heidi got into her car, she pulled out her cell phone and called her parents. Fortunately they were home. She asked them to call the Turners and find out Mr. Cobb's home phone number, then call her back.

Halfway to San Diego, she heard from her father, who gave her the number. She phoned immediately, and it didn't surprise her to get the attorney's voice mail. On a late Sunday afternoon he could be anywhere.

"Mr. Cobb? This is Heidi Ellis, Dana's friend. I've just been to the prison to visit her. She needs medication for her claustrophobia. Surely something can be done to help her with that. But more importantly, we've got to get her out." Her voice trembled as she spoke.

"Dana doesn't belong in there. She's not going to last very long. I'd like to reopen the case. If you'd get back to me at home and tell me what has to be done to make that happen, I'd be very grateful.

"I'm going to be frank. If you feel you can't do any more for her, please let me know so my family and I can retain another attorney.

"Please call me as soon as you can. I don't care how late it is. Thank you very much."

Heidi gave him the number at her apartment and ended the call.

It felt good to have done that much, but when she hadn't heard from Mr. Cobb by the time she'd returned to San Diego, she was frantic.

Unable to concentrate, she drove to her parents' home in Mission Bay. Decisions needed to be made as soon as possible. Every minute that passed drained more of the life out of her friend.

IT WAS TEN AFTER NINE Thursday night as Gideon Poletti approached the nursing station. "Can you tell me which room you've put Daniel Mcfarlane? He asked to see me."

The registered nurse on the oncology wing at St. Anne's looked up from a chart. "He's in west-160. Please keep your visit short. He has surgery in the morning."

"That's what I heard."

While he'd been following up a lead in a missing person case, Gideon had received a phone call from Ellen Mcfarlane. Her husband, Gideon's former boss, was in the hospital with prostate cancer.

Last year everyone in local law enforcement had gone through a hard time accepting the retirement of the brilliant, shrewd head of the San Diego Homicide division. The city had lost a great warrior.

Though another qualified detective with years of service in every department had been installed to head the division, it would be impossible to fill the older man's shoes.

Gideon had always been good friends with Daniel, both on and off the job. But the older man had made himself scarce since his retirement, and Gideon hadn't seen him in several months.

Following the arrows to the west wing, he found the room in question. Ellen was at her husband's bedside. For a man about to undergo surgery, Daniel appeared as vibrant as ever. Unlike a lot of men in their late sixties, he still had most of his dark hair, which was finely streaked with silver.

"Gideon!" He sat up in the bed. "I'm glad you could make it."

"I came as soon as I could."

He hugged Ellen, who excused herself so the two men could talk. Then Gideon shook Daniel's hand before pulling up a chair next to the bed.

"I'm sorry to hear about your illness."

"So am I." The older man chuckled. "But the doc assures me the surgery's routine and I'll be my old self in no time. I've decided to believe him."

"I believe it, too, Daniel. Now, what can I do for you?"

A sheepish expression crossed the older man's face, something Gideon had never seen before. He had a premonition that his friend was about to ask him an unusual favor.

"If you can't or don't want to help me out, all you have to do is say so. It would mean some sacrifice on your par—"

"Daniel," Gideon interrupted him. His curiosity had reached its peak. "What is it?"

"All right. As soon as I retired, I was besieged with requests for speaking engagements, teaching seminars, interviews, you name it. I was even offered a university position.''

Gideon nodded. "I can imagine.''

"I turned everything down because of a promise I made to my wife. We've spent most of this year traveling or vacationing at our cabin in Oregon.

"Then a few weeks ago I got a call from the local school district asking me to teach an adult community education class on criminology. My daughter, Kathie, is a teacher serving on that board, and she put them up to it. I think she's worried that her old man's missing the department.''

"I think she's probably right.''

Daniel smiled. "Yes and no. I'm working on a book, which I'm enjoying very much. But I won't lie to you. There are times I miss the old adrenaline rush.

"However, that's not the point. Because of Kathie, I said I'd teach one class. The first session was last night. But this morning my doctor phoned the house with the results of some tests taken last week. He said he wanted me to come in and have the surgery immediately.''

Gideon could see where this was headed.

"Tomorrow night's the next class. The spring quarter runs for six weeks, and the classes are on Wednesday and Friday evenings from seven to nine. If all goes well, I'll be able to finish up the last six classes or so. But I need someone to fill in for me for the rest of April and part of May. You're the man I want to take my place.''

"I'm not a teacher, Daniel.''

"Neither am I,'' Daniel said with a grin. "All you'd

have to do is pretend you're investigating a murder. Proceed as if you were in charge of the crime scene. Just verbalize the steps so they'll know what you're thinking and doing. Emphasize forensics—the class is particularly interested in that. That's it!''

"Not quite. I'm not the legendary Daniel Mcfarlane.''

Daniel ignored that comment. "Before you say no, Gideon, hear me out. My daughter's built me up to be some kind of paragon, which I'm not. However I do know a man who is, and that's *you.*''

"Come on," Gideon scoffed.

"It's the truth. The day you resigned from the NYPD to move to San Diego and join the force was our good fortune. Right from the start you were the officer who stood out from the rest. Over the years you've distinguished yourself again and again. The way you helped bring down that Russian Mafia ring last fall was damned impressive.''

"Don't give me the credit, Daniel. My friend Max Calder is the one who deserves it.''

"I agree it was a team effort. Nevertheless, because of your undercover work with the FBI, the powers that be were considering you to take my place. But they don't like to promote any detective to that position until he's at least forty-five.''

By now Gideon was on his feet. "I would never want your old job. Not only could no one else ever measure up, Kevin needs me around on a regular basis. Serving on that special task force took a year out of my life and made it difficult to spend enough time with him. He's been much happier since I went back on regular assignment.''

"That's the beauty of this class. If it's Kevin's night for visitation, he could go with you and do his homework at the back of the room.''

Gideon grunted. "You're a sly old fox, Mcfarlane. Go on. I'm still listening.''

"You'd be teaching ten mystery writers, most of them women.''

His wink didn't fool Gideon, who'd been divorced for ten years now. Daniel had been after him to get married again. But Gideon had his own ideas about that. His ex-wife's betrayal had caused a lot of damage.

Finding out he wasn't Kevin's biological father until Fay asked him for a divorce had killed something inside Gideon. Though he eventually started dating again, he was content with his bachelor status. His son meant everything to him.

"A couple of these writers are already published,'' Daniel explained. "Several seem to be on the verge. Kathie's counting on me, so I want the best detective on the force teaching this group. How about it?''

There was no way Gideon could turn Daniel down. They'd been friends and colleagues for too long.

"I tell you what,'' Gideon said. "I'll check with the sergeant to make certain I'm free on those nights. When he hears that you're the reason for the request, I'm sure I won't have a problem. The important thing is for you to get well.''

"Thanks, Gideon. They're a nice group. Tomorrow night they'll be bringing their latest ideas for a mystery. I gave them an assignment. They'll each have two minutes—no more—to present a synopsis they've been working on. I told them I'd pick the one that intrigued me the most, and we'd start there."

"Where's the class?"

"Mesa Junior High in Mission Beach."

"I was there last year for one of Kevin's soccer games."

"Just go to the main office a few minutes before seven. Larry Johnson runs the adult-education classes. He'll have an attendance roll and room key."

"All right. I'll take care of it. Now I'd better leave. The nurse told me to make this brief. I think I've already overstayed my welcome."

The older man smiled his thanks. "I owe you for this. Naturally you'll be compensated." He sighed in obvious relief. "You have no idea how much I appreciate this."

Gideon knew. This class might seem a minor obligation to most people, but Daniel took his commitments seriously. So did Gideon.

He got to his feet and grasped Daniel's shoulder firmly. "I'm glad to help out. Take care and mind the doctor. I'll check back with you tomorrow."

The two men shook hands once more, and then Gideon left the room. Daniel's wife was coming down the hall.

"Don't worry about anything, Ellen. I told him I'd take over his class until he's on his feet again."

"Bless you," she murmured as they hugged goodbye. "Daniel thinks the world of you. He wouldn't even consider anyone else."

"That's nice to hear. Your husband's tough. He'll pull through this and he'll be better than ever."

"I hope you're right."

"I know I am. I'll call in the morning for an update."

"Please do. His surgery is scheduled for 6:00 a.m."

"Good. It'll be over before you know it."

Gideon left the hospital and headed for his house in Ocean Beach. En route he phoned his supervisor to see what could be arranged.

Since the divorce when Kevin was three, Wednesdays had been set aside for the boy's midweek visitation with Gideon. The decree also allowed visitation every other weekend, every other holiday and six weeks every summer.

It had never been enough for Gideon, but Fay had remarried within months of their divorce. Because of her desire that Kevin bond with his new stepfather, she'd refused to deviate from the stipulations set by the court.

Not wanting to cause any more trauma to their son, Gideon had accepted the situation. He believed children needed their mothers. But now that Kevin was in eighth grade, he was begging to live with Gideon fulltime.

Kevin didn't dislike his stepfather, but he'd never developed any real affection for him. Of course, the boy loved his mother, but she and her husband were both busy stockbrokers. Kevin had been raised by a series of nannies until he started junior high. Then there'd been a string of baby-sitters.

That was the problem.

According to Gideon's attorney, Kevin was now old enough to choose which parent he wanted to live with. But Fay would be impossible if Kevin moved in with Gideon. She would heap enough guilt on their son to traumatize him.

In the long run Gideon felt it was better to leave things as they were.

Gideon had explained all this to Kevin, who'd cried quietly, then clung to him, vowing that the day he turned eighteen he was going to come and live with his father.

They *were* father and son, no matter that Kevin's biological father was some high-powered stockbroker from New York who had no idea he had a child.

Unbeknownst to Gideon, Fay had slept with her boss while she was engaged to Gideon. Afraid to tell him the truth, she'd passed the baby off as Gideon's. After almost four years of marriage, she got involved with another stockbroker in San Diego and then asked Gideon for a divorce.

Though he'd known his wife was always striving for something he couldn't seem to give her, he hadn't realized she'd gone as far as to have an affair.

Shocked by her refusal to try to keep their marriage together through counseling, he sued for custody of Kevin. That was when he learned about her previous affair. A DNA test confirmed that Kevin wasn't Gideon's son.

When the judge heard the case, he decreed that Gideon was Kevin's father in all the ways that mattered and granted him the most liberal visitation rights under the law.

Unless Fay softened, which would probably never happen, there was nothing to do but go on making the best of a situation Gideon would never have wished on an innocent child. He certainly wasn't about to tell his son he was another man's child. It wasn't information Kevin needed to know. Gideon had consulted several counselors at the time of the divorce, and they all agreed.

There *was* a bright side to Daniel's request for help. Gideon would take his suggestion and bring Kevin to class on the visitation nights. His son had always been curious about Gideon's work. He could do his homework and listen at the same time. They'd have dinner either before class or after and make a special night of it.

Once school was out at the end of May, Kevin would be spending the first half of the summer with Gideon. This year they were going to vacation in Alaska for a couple of weeks and do some salmon fishing with Max and his wife, Gaby.

Since his marriage, Max had resigned from the FBI and was now a detective in the same division of the San Diego Police Department as Gideon. It was a little like the old days, when the two of them had been rookie cops together in New York. Only this was much better because those dark days of pain and lies were behind them both.

Fortunately Kevin had always been crazy about Max. Now he was equally crazy about Gaby, who was expecting a child in August. Already Gideon's son had volunteered to baby-sit. Kevin's happiness was all that mattered to Gideon these days.

BY FRIDAY MORNING Heidi had reached an all-time
low. Mr. Cobb's office had indicated that he was out
of the country and wouldn't return before Sunday
night. On Thursday she'd taken a personal-leave day
from school to spend time with her parents while they
discussed what to do about Dana's situation.

After much soul-searching, Heidi decided she'd have
to wait until she could talk to Mr. Cobb before she
asked her father to get hold of that other attorney. It
was the only honorable thing to do. But it was hard to
wait when she knew a week with no news was like a
year to Dana.

When Heidi arrived at school on Friday morning, she
felt emotionally exhausted. Without much enthusiasm,
she went through the stack of mail and flyers that had
accumulated in her teacher's box over two days. After
scanning each piece, she tossed most of them in the
wastebasket, then hurried out of the main office to her
room at the end of the west hall.

The first bell at Mesa Junior High in Mission Beach
wouldn't ring for half an hour. She breathed a sigh of
relief to know she had thirty more minutes to get the
room ready for class.

Six years of teaching had taught her to present new
geography units to her ninth-graders on Thursdays.
That way, the kids who thought the weekend started
on Friday morning couldn't use the excuse that they'd
missed the initial presentation. But she'd had to make
an exception and stay home yesterday because Dana's
problems had superceded anything else.

Now that fourth term of the school year had started,
it was time to cover the Middle East, an area so foreign

to most of her students they had no clue it wasn't another neighborhood in San Diego.

Her classes included a pretty-equal mix of Asian, African-American, Hispanic and white students. Her goal was that by the time school was out, they could each, on a map of the world, place the oceans, continents, countries and major cities.

After she'd unlocked the door to her room, the first thing she noticed was the writing on the front board.

Rule 1. Never assume anything!

She frowned. The information she'd put on the board for the substitute had been erased. Why?

She glanced at her books and papers, which had been rearranged on top of her desk. That was odd. All the substitutes who'd ever taught for her had always left everything exactly as they'd found it.

Wondering what was going on, she rang the office, using the switch on the wall behind her desk. One of the secretaries answered.

"This is Sheila. What can I do for you?"

"Hi, Sheila. It's Heidi. You wouldn't happen to know who subbed for me yesterday, would you?"

"Yes. That huge teachers' seminar in the district drained all the subs, so different teachers from our building took your classes on their free periods and let the kids do any homework they wanted. Is there a problem?"

"No, I was just surprised that my lesson plan was erased from the board."

"That's probably because the community school just started their adult classes. Mr. Johnson arranged the schedule. He's put someone in your room on Wednesday and Friday nights from seven to eight-thirty. Just a sec and I'll see who it is.

"Okay—found it. The teacher's name is Mcfarlane. According to this, the class is an introduction to criminology."

Criminology?

Her heart gave a strange thud.

"If you don't want him in there, I'll ask another teacher."

"No! No—don't do that!" *Please, don't do that. Maybe this is the answer to my prayers.* "I'd forgotten about community school." All the teachers had to take turns sharing their rooms.

"You're sure it's okay?"

"Positive."

"Mr. Johnson says that if any of you have complaints, you should put a note in his box and he'll talk to the person. They've been told to leave the rooms exactly as they find them. If you're missing anything, I'll send a student aide with the supplies you need."

"Thanks, Sheila, but I'm fine. I just had to make sure I didn't have a bunch of gremlins in here."

The other woman snorted inelegantly. "Sometimes adults are worse than the kids."

They both chuckled, but in reality it wasn't very funny.

"Sheila, will you ask one of your aides to get me a list of the teachers who watched my classes yesterday? I want to thank them."

"Sure thing."

"Talk to you later."

She shut off the switch, then wrote an outline of the

material to be covered in the Middle East unit on the board. But the entire time she was writing, her mind dwelled on the words she'd just erased.

Rule 1. Never assume anything!

Heidi's thoughts went back to that excruciatingly painful day in late August when she'd learned the dreadful news. Based on circumstantial evidence, the jury had assumed Dana was guilty of first-degree murder. The judge gave her a thirty-year prison sentence for killing Amy.

Ever since Heidi had found out that her friend had been convicted of a crime she didn't commit, the joy had gone out of her life. Many times since that day, Heidi had talked with Dana's parents about getting the case reopened, but there'd been no new evidence. Mr. Cobb's hands were tied. Now Dana herself had lost all hope.

Heidi couldn't blame her or her parents for feeling so utterly defeated. That was why someone outside the Turner family had to pursue other avenues for them. Heidi was that person.

She frequently wished she was an attorney who had the legal know-how to begin an investigation of her own. She'd give anything to find evidence that would prove her friend's innocence.

If that criminology class could be of any help at all…

By the time she realized how far her tortured thoughts had wandered, the second bell had rung, and the student-body officers had already started announcements over the PA system.

"Hi, everybody. We want to congratulate our girls'

volleyball team for their great win yesterday against Clairemont. Way to go, Mesa! Let's all get out and support our girls next week for their big game against Torrey Pines.

"This next announcement concerns the social-studies service project scheduled for today. Those students whose last names start with A to M, will go this morning. The buses will be outside the building in fifteen meetings. Teachers, please take attendance. We'll call the students down when it's time to board."

That announcement affected about a third of Heidi's class. She'd already signed all their permission slips to help plant trees at a new senior citizens' facility. Unfortunately she'd forgotten.

If truth be known, she'd forgotten a lot of things. After her talk with Dana last Sunday, she'd come back so weighed down with pain for her friend it had been difficult to concentrate or feel enthusiasm for anything.

After the announcements Heidi said, "Good morning, students. Those of you leaving on the bus will have just enough time to copy the material from the board. No one is exempt from tonight's assignment, so let's get busy."

The class moaned, but they knew she meant business and settled down to work. All the while they were writing, Heidi's mind was on her friend. No matter how many times she tried to put herself in Dana's place, she couldn't.

The more she thought about it, the more she felt it would be worth attending the night class in criminology that was being held in her room. At least it was a place to start, to ask questions. Heidi didn't know how much longer she could stand to watch her friend waste away. Especially with the real murderer still out there.

Six hours later she locked the door to her room and hurried through the crowded halls to the community-education office. Larry Johnson's secretary was still at her desk.

"Carol?"

The other woman looked up and smiled. "Hello, stranger. Haven't seen you since the Christmas party when you were with that medical student you were dating. I heard it was pretty serious."

"I thought he might be the one, Carol, but it didn't work out."

Jeff Madsen hadn't been able to handle Heidi's pre-occupation with Dana's murder case. Maybe it was too much to ask of a man who was overwhelmed with studies and hospital rotations. In any event, the meaning went out of their relationship. He stopped calling as often. She stopped caring. One day she woke up and realized it was over.

"Well, you know what they say—you're lucky to have escaped a situation that wasn't meant to be. I went through your experience several times before I got married. Mark my words. Some terrific guy is still out there searching for you."

"I hope." The breakup with Jeff had taken its toll. But even worse was Dana's imprisonment, which had robbed Heidi of any potential for happiness.

"With your looks, are you kidding?"

"It's nice of you to say that, Carol."

"I only speak the truth." She sighed. "Okay. You

must've had a reason to come in here when school's already out for the day.''

Heidi nodded. "I'd like to sign up for the night class being held in my room.''

She rolled her eyes. "You and a thousand others.''

"Really?''

"We've got a genuine VIP teaching this term.''

"Sheila told me it was a Mr. Mcfarlane.''

"It's *the* Daniel Mcfarlane. He retired last year as head of Homicide at the San Diego Police Department. The man has more commendations than a five-star general.

"His daughter's on the community-ed board, so we were the only school in this city lucky enough to get him to teach a criminology class. It's a one-time deal. Everyone's been trying to get in.

"The bad news is, he stipulated ten people max. Those spots filled up within five minutes. Sorry.''

CHAPTER TWO

THE CLASS WAS FULL!

Heidi couldn't believe how upset she was by the news. All day she'd been counting on being able to attend. The more she'd thought about it, the more she'd realized this was exactly what she needed if she wanted to learn how to investigate a crime.

According to Carol, it was the only criminology class being taught in the entire school district. She must have moaned aloud because the other woman said, "I wish I didn't have to turn you down. However, I do have an idea..."

"I think I have the same idea, Carol, but it wouldn't be fair to hang around in my room tonight on the pretext that I've got work to do."

"Then just talk to him before class. Ask him if he'd consider letting in one more. You never know."

Yes, she decided. That was exactly what she'd do. "You're right. I'll try it. Thanks."

Back in her room, she cleaned the board and set up the chairs in a semicircle for the night class. Then she left school and hurried home to eat and get ready to come back.

At quarter after six, she pulled into the school's parking lot and rushed into the building again.

She didn't want Mr. Mcfarlane to know it was her classroom he was using, since she didn't want to put any undue pressure on him. Her plan was to wait in the hall until he showed up. At that point she'd prevail on him to let her be part of his group. If he agreed, she'd tell him how she'd found out about the night class.

A few people had entered the building ahead of her. Heidi walked past the main office to the west wing but slowed down when she saw that her door was already open.

She checked her watch. The man was forty minutes early for his class. If he'd come ahead of time to prepare, he might not like being disturbed.

After a slight hesitation, she peered around the edge of the door. Her eyes widened in surprise as she saw a rugged-looking man in his midthirties writing something on the board. He had to be six foot two or three, with wavy dark-brown hair cut fairly short. The navy business suit, toned with a royal blue shirt, couldn't disguise his hard-muscled physique.

Heidi found herself staring at him in fascination.

He couldn't possibly be the retired investigator Carol had raved about.

Her spirits fell. An older man might be more malleable. Heidi didn't know what to think about this stranger.

Maybe Mr. Mcfarlane couldn't come tonight and had sent a substitute. In that case, it was possible his replacement wouldn't let Heidi sit in on the class. Then again, he could simply be an assistant and Mr. Mcfarlane would arrive shortly. All she had to do was go in the room and her questions would be answered.

After another minute of watching him, she realized how embarrassing it would be if he happened to glance in the direction of the door and saw her eyeing him with such frank pleasure.

Gathering her courage, she walked in. When he looked over, she momentarily held her breath. Between thick dark lashes glowed a pair of brilliant blue eyes the same hue as his shirt. They swept over her in guarded male admiration.

"Hello," they said simultaneously.

He smiled and put down the chalk. "Hi. I'm Detective Gideon Poletti."

"I'm Heidi Ellis."

His narrowed gaze wandered over her hair and face. It set her pulse racing. "Your name's not on the list."

"No. I came early to see if I could join the class," she said, hating that she sounded out of breath. "I guess I'll have to wait to speak to Mr. Mcfarlane."

"He had surgery this morning and won't be able to teach for at least a month."

"Oh, no!" She bit her lip to prevent the tears that threatened the moment he'd said Mr. Mcfarlane wouldn't be coming. She'd been counting on this opportunity to try to help Dana, long shot though it was. These days her emotions hovered near the surface. There was little she could do to hide them.

The detective eyed her with concern. "I can understand your disappointment. Daniel's a legend in this part of the state. Unfortunately he needed to find a substitute and asked me to do the honors. I could never hope to fill his shoes, but you're welcome to join the class.''

"Thank you," she whispered. "Thank you very much. Please don't think my reaction had anything to do with you personally. It's just that I was hoping he'd let me in. And then when I realized someone else had come, I wasn't sure, and—"

"You don't have to worry," he assured her before she could finish. "Welcome to the class."

Grateful for his willingness to add her to the group, she shook the hand he extended. Hers became enveloped in a strong grip. Warmth spread through her body before he released it. She wondered if he'd experienced the same tingling sensation.

When he let her go, he said, "Take any seat in the semicircle. It looks like the teacher who's here during the day went to the trouble of setting things up for this class. I'll have to find a way to thank whoever it was."

"You already have," came her tremulous reply.

He blinked as realization dawned. "This is your room?"

"Guilty as charged. That's how I learned about the criminology class. Mr. Mcfarlane left something written on the board Wednesday night."

His lips twitched in amusement. "What did it say?"

"'Rule 1. Never assume anything.'"

"That sounds like Dan."

"You know him well?"

"He was my boss until his retirement last year."

She couldn't tear her eyes away from the intensity of his. "If he chose you to replace him, then it means this class is very fortunate."

I'm very fortunate, she thought. *Maybe you'll be able to help me.*

"I don't follow."

"Considering his reputation, I'm sure Mr. Mcfarlane wouldn't have asked you to take over for him unless he thought you were the best."

"That would be nice if it were true."

The man's charm was already working on her. "Thanks again for allowing me to participate. I'll pay at the community-ed office after class."

"That's fine." He moved to her desk and handed her the attendance sheet. She noticed he didn't wear a wedding ring. "Why don't you add your name. Be sure to put a home phone number next to it, in case I need to get in touch with you. I'm not anticipating any emergencies, but you never know."

Heidi took it from him. There were phone numbers written by the names of the other class members. It was ridiculous, but for just a moment she'd hoped he'd wanted hers for personal reasons.

GIDEON TURNED AND FINISHED writing information on the board. It was important he keep himself occupied until the rest of the class arrived. Otherwise he might be tempted to stare at the schoolteacher sitting only a few feet away.

There was only one word to describe her. *Knockout.* The woman was a knockout.

Short and curvy, she had gleaming red-gold hair to her shoulders and blue eyes that lightened or darkened depending on her emotions. He imagined that every boy lucky enough to be in her class had a terrible crush on her.

She was like the most scintillating ornament on the Christmas tree, the one that drew your gaze again and again.

They'd spoken only a few words, yet he already felt the impact of her personality and was excited by it. How many years had it been since he'd sensed a real connection to a woman on first meeting?

Her room was as exciting as she was. He liked the idea that this was her world. It told him a lot about her. Artifacts and posters from every continent had been mounted on the walls with a decorator's flair.

Her furniture wasn't standard school issue. She'd had this large mahogany desk brought in, along with a small brass desk lamp, a comfortable padded leather chair and an Oriental rug, of all things, in shades of deep blue and green.

There were several small potted trees surrounded by a dozen potted flowering plants. She'd created a setting of warmth and comfort. No schoolroom he'd ever sat in had looked like this.

It all appealed to him. *She* appealed to him. Without conscious thought he let his eyes wander to her hair, which seemed to have a life of its own.

She didn't wear a wedding ring, which was surprising. Any woman as utterly feminine and desirable as she was should have been claimed by some fortunate man a long time ago. Maybe she was living with somebody, though.

Since the divorce, Gideon had been operating in deep-freeze mode where the opposite sex was concerned. It was shocking to discover he could be this affected by a five-foot-two female he would have to pick up in his arms in order to properly kiss.

"Ladies and gentlemen," came a male voice over the PA system, jerking Gideon from private thoughts he hadn't entertained in a long, long time. "I'm Larry Johnson, head of the adult-education program for the northern region. Welcome to Mesa Junior High. It's seven o'clock, time for class to start.

"In case you're having trouble finding your room, please stop by the community-ed office in the main foyer. We have maps of the building. There will be no bell rung for a break to use the rest rooms or get a drink of water. That will be at the discretion of each teacher.

"At eight-thirty a bell will ring to signal the end of the class. If you have business with the office, Carol Sargent, the secretary, will be here until nine. A reminder to teachers—please drop by the office with your attendance rolls before you leave the building tonight. Enjoy your evening."

While Gideon had been lost in thought, the rest of the class had entered the room. When he turned around, he discovered that every chair in the semicircle had been taken.

Two men and eight women were looking at him with expectant expressions, waiting for an explanation. Nine women if you counted the attractive newcomer who seemed less carefree than the others. He couldn't forget the disappointment in her eyes when he'd told her Daniel wouldn't be teaching the class.

"Good evening. I'm Detective Poletti, but you can

call me Gideon. I work for the Homicide division of the San Diego Police Department.

"I hate to be the bearer of bad news, but I'm afraid Lieutenant Mcfarlane had to undergo emergency surgery this morning. His wife told me it went very well, and the doctor estimates he'll be back teaching this class by mid-May at the latest. But for the time being, you're stuck with me."

He imagined he could hear their collective sigh of disappointment, even though they didn't make a sound.

"No one understands more than I do how you feel about that announcement. When I left the New York City Police Department and moved here fourteen years ago, I was made a detective and assigned to Lieutenant Mcfarlane's office.

"There aren't many people in law enforcement who have his brilliance and instincts. His reputation for solving crimes is unequaled. I was lucky enough to work under him until he retired last year. With Daniel gone, I can tell you there's a void in the department that will never be filled.

"Having said that, life has to go on. Daniel asked me if I'd teach this class until his return. I'm prepared to honor his wishes, but I won't take it personally if you'd prefer to drop out and take the class again when he can be here."

A hand shot up. It was the redhead's.

"Yes, Ms. Ellis?"

"Heidi, please. This is my first night here, and I can't speak for the others...but I don't intend to drop this class. I've been looking forward to it." The throb in her voice was echoed in her eyes.

The others sounded equally enthusiastic in their concurrence, but he hardly noticed because he was still reacting to her declaration.

Just as he had a few minutes ago, when she'd seemed almost desperate to join the class, he sensed an urgency behind her request that went beyond sheer interest. He wasn't so egotistical that he believed she felt a personal attraction to him. That was no more than wishful thinking.

His instincts, which had been refined over years of detective work, were telling him she had something at stake here. That in itself intrigued him. He wanted to find out what she was after.

He also wanted to find out if she was involved with anyone.

After marking everyone present, he said, "Thank you for your faith in me. Daniel told me I'd like this class. I have to admit I'm looking forward to teaching you the fundamentals of solving a crime. I'll probably enjoy it a lot more than you will, for the simple reason that for once, I won't be dealing with a real homicide."

At those words everyone laughed—except Heidi Ellis, who averted her eyes. Before Gideon went home tonight, he intended to discover what was going on inside her beautiful head.

"I understand that your assignment was to bring a synopsis of a mystery you're planning to write. At the end of class I'll collect them. Over the weekend, I'll read through them and make comments before I pass them back.

"For now, why don't you get them out and we'll start the oral presentations. Two minutes each should be long enough to give the class an idea of your basic plot.

"I'll refrain from making comments about your stories until everyone's had an opportunity to speak. At that point, I'll let you know which mystery I think we should pursue as a class. Mr. Riley?"

"Call me Bob."

"Okay, Bob. I can see you're ready to go. Let's begin with you. Come up here so everyone can hear you."

The other man lumbered to the front of the room. "My story is about a serial killer in Houston, Texas, who wants to get back at the female teacher who humiliated him in class."

Startled by the unexpected beginning, Heidi glanced up, and her eyes happened to meet Gideon's. They both smiled. It was a private moment, over within seconds, yet he'd felt a connection with her that was even stronger than before.

"His hatred is so great that later on in life, he gets a job as a painter for the Houston school board.

"This man now has the freedom to enter any public school at any time and case it without being suspected. He picks his opportunity, then strangles his victim, who is always a female teacher. His original teacher has long since retired, but he doesn't care about that. Ten teachers are killed before he's caught."

Gideon's eyes met Heidi's once more, then he thanked Bob and asked the woman seated next to him, Nancy to come up and read her synopsis.

"I'm really nervous, you guys, so don't laugh. My story is about two world-class skiers, a guy and a girl, training in Vail, Colorado. They've lived together for six months and share a room at the hotel where the American team is staying.

"But their relationship has been plagued by violent arguments. She accuses him of not being interested in her career and wanting all the fame for himself. He accuses her of sleeping around.

"One morning after completing their first run, they go up on the double chairlift to start the second. Halfway to the top of the mountain, she falls out of the chair. Steve is horrified but can't do anything until he's let off at the top so he can ski down to her.

"By the time he reaches her, she's dead. There's an inquest, and it's determined that Steve pushed her to her death. He maintains that he's innocent, that he was in love with her. But the facts suggest otherwise."

Nancy looked at Gideon. "That's all I have so far."

"That's fine. Next let's hear from Patricia."

"Call me Pat," she said after taking Nancy's place. "This is my very first story, so it's not really thought out the way the others have been. I want to write a novel about this nurse who kills people on life support because she thinks she's doing them a favor.

"I'm a nurse, so I feel comfortable about writing a murder mystery set in a hospital. There are a lot of suspects, including this one doctor she's in love with and…"

HEIDI SAT THROUGH the next fifteen minutes of scenarios, still warmed by the detective's smile. She'd thought him attractive the moment she'd caught sight of him from the hallway. But the amusement reflected in his face and eyes had made him totally irresistible—the kind of man you rarely met in real life. The chances of his being single and unattached were a million to one, she thought with resignation.

"Heidi?" He called on her last. "If you're a writer, perhaps you'd like to share an idea for a mystery novel with the class."

She lifted her head. Again she found herself gazing into eyes as blue as the ocean after the sun has burned off the haze.

Afraid it would sound suspicious if she stood up and gave a perfect outline of Dana's case without the aid of notes, she said, "I wasn't here for the first class to get the assignment. So if it's all right, I'll bring a synopsis next week."

No one needed to know she wasn't a writer. She figured that most, if not all, of the people in this room held a job and did writing in their spare time. For the next while she preferred to stay in the background; she'd wait to see what comments he'd make about her synopsis once she'd handed it in next Wednesday.

She hated any delay, but she was afraid to talk to him about Dana's case so soon. After all, this was the detective's first night teaching the class. She couldn't risk alienating him right off the bat by asking for preferential treatment, not when an opportunity like this had finally come her way.

The detective eyed her for a moment, as if pondering her response. Then he got out of his chair to stand in front of them, legs slightly apart. Heidi tried not to be aware of his arresting masculinity, but it was impossible.

"Every story I heard would make a fascinating mystery, but I'm not an editor. My job is to turn you into professional sleuths in ten easy lessons—at least in your imaginations." He flashed the class a quick smile that made Heidi's heart falter briefly.

"On Wednesday night you learned that you must never assume anything. After hearing from everyone this evening, you can see why. Although we knew who the culprit was in all but one of the stories—Nancy's— our minds were busy conceiving of any number of suspects who would've been capable of committing the crime. No doubt many of you would've chosen another character to be the culprit."

Heidi nodded with the class. That was exactly what she'd done.

"How many of you have ever eaten a pastry called a Napoleon?"

Several hands went up, including Heidi's.

"The French call them *mille feuilles*. A thousand leaves. The pastry is made up of many layers. A mystery is like that. As soon as you expose one layer, you find another, then another. Leaf by leaf, you carefully examine what you find.

"You subject the crime scene to thorough analysis. You follow up on every lead. You never leave a question unanswered, even if it takes you months, years or in some cases, all your life."

Heidi shivered. He'd just zeroed in on her thoughts. Even if it took the rest of her life, she would never stop doing everything she could to see her friend go free.

"If some small point nags at you," the detective

continued, ''you listen to your intuition and rethink it, rework it, until you've satisfied your curiosity.

''When I'm called to a crime scene, I try to keep an open mind, no matter how strongly I might be persuaded that a certain suspect has to be guilty because of circumstantial evidence.

''Consider Nancy's story about the skier who was blamed for pushing his girlfriend to her death. We weren't given a lot of information, yet based on the fact that he was sitting next to her, he had opportunity. We know he was jealous, so he certainly had motive.

''I don't know how Nancy plans to finish her story, but by the time this class is through, she'll understand what goes on at a crime scene. Armed with that information, I'm betting she'll have come up with any number of alternative explanations.

''The victim might have been on drugs and fallen by accident. Or she could have decided to commit suicide—for any of a number of reasons. She might have hated her boyfriend enough to kill herself and hope he got blamed for it.

''Maybe she was pregnant with another skier's baby and didn't want her coach to know because he'd throw her off the team. Maybe she was pregnant with her boyfriend's baby and didn't want *him* to know. Or maybe she was afraid that if he knew, he'd insist she give up skiing.

''Possibly she jumped intending to kill the baby but not herself. Then again, maybe the bar holding the skiers in the chair gave way, and it was an accident, pure and simple. Especially if there was enough wind to make the chair sway and send her plunging before her boyfriend could prevent it.''

''I love that explanation!'' Nancy cried out.

While everyone laughed and began a lively discussion of which version they felt she should use, Heidi thought back to Dana's case. According to Dr. Turner, the prosecuting attorney had called it an open-and-shut case. A question of sibling rivalry that turned to jealousy, then murder.

But listening to Detective Poletti suggesting one possibility after another for the fictional skier's death underscored Heidi's belief that the police had overlooked something vital in Dana's case. Something that would point to the real killer.

''Before I tell you which of your stories I've picked for the class to analyze, I'm going to pass out a packet detailing a homicide that happened in San Francisco a few years ago.

''This case will be your textbook. Inside is an incident report, crime-scene evidence reports, coroner's report and a press report revealing the arrests made after a two-month investigation. Go ahead and look through it. Then you're free to get up and stretch or use the washrooms at either end of the hall. We'll reconvene in five minutes.''

Only the man named Tom left the room. The others immersed themselves in the information the detective had distributed. Heidi glanced through the pages, but her mind was still on Dana.

How she wished it was her friend's case they were studying!

As soon as Tom was back, the teacher asked each

of them to make one observation about what they'd read. Everyone said the same thing. They had no idea so much evidence *could* be gathered at a crime scene.

The detective nodded. "Perhaps now you'll understand why many criminal cases fail to stand up in court. If the investigating officers overlook a piece of vital evidence, or if someone purposely or unwittingly disturbs the crime scene and tampers with the evidence before a team of experts can get in there, crucial bits of information are lost.

"It's unfortunate that, on occasion, the police themselves have been accused of tainting or even planting evidence, but we're not going to get into that in this class.

"Okay, let's proceed to the mystery we'll be examining. We'll assume the crime scene is untouched and waiting for Mesa Junior High's detectives to begin their investigation."

A ripple of excitement swept through the room.

Heidi hadn't met Mr. Mcfarlane, but she couldn't imagine him enthralling the class the way Detective Poletti had. The man possessed so much genuine charm and charisma, everyone was mesmerized.

In fact, she couldn't think of another man who exuded such confidence and intelligence without being at all overbearing. As she looked around, she realized the men, as well as the women, were captivated by his personality and easygoing manner.

"Emily Deerborn? I've chosen your synopsis."

Everyone clapped for the beaming older woman and told her how lucky she was that her story had been the one selected.

The detective said, "Why don't we ask Heidi to read it for us this time? When she's finished, someone tell the class why I decided this was a good mystery for us to study."

Heidi already knew why. Or at least she thought she knew. After she'd done her part, she sat down. At that point several hands went up, but their answers weren't what he was looking for. Heidi raised hers.

His gaze swerved in her direction. "What's your guess, Heidi?"

"A lot of the other stories dealt with motives that would have to be explored by interviewing suspects and witnesses alike. This story involved a poisoning carried out by four culprits. That means there's an unusual amount of physical evidence that will have to be gathered in order for all four to be arrested in the end."

Something flickered in the depths of his eyes. "I couldn't have said it better myself. Emily has presented a case in which forensics will play a vital role. Daniel told me you signed up for this class to learn more about forensic science."

Just as everyone nodded and made comments, the bell rang.

He glanced at his watch. "It's time to go. Here's your assignment."

They all opened their notebooks and started writing.

"Over the weekend I want you to put on your detective hats. You'll be writing up Emily's incident report. I'll start you off.

"It's a Tuesday morning. You've been called to the scene of a possible homicide. You enter the office building with another detective and find two police officers, as well as two paramedics, already there, along with one witness who works in that office.

"Said witness came to work and discovered her boss slumped over the desk, so she called 911.

"With that scene in mind, list as many things as you can think of that need to be done on the spot. Use the textbook case I gave you to help make your list. Wednesday, we'll put everything on the board and go from there.

"As you leave the room, please put your synopsis on the desk. Make sure your name's on it."

The class members got out of their seats and clustered around Detective Poletti. When he went into the hall, they followed, bombarding him with questions. Heidi hurriedly rearranged the desks for Monday morning.

She would have erased the board where he'd written his name and an outline of the class, but he came back inside and did it for her.

"Thank you."

"You're welcome." His eyes were smiling and alive. "What else can I do for you?"

"Not a thing. I'm ready to go. I need to pay my fee for the class before the secretary goes home."

"Since I have to hand in the attendance roll, I'll walk with you."

He waited while she turned out lights and locked the door, then they started down the hall. Her awareness of him made it difficult to act naturally.

Jeff had been a much shorter man with an average build. Detective Poletti's tall, well-honed frame was a revelation.

The last thing she wanted was to act like some of the other women in the class who'd already made their attraction to him obvious.

"You weren't a detective in another life, were you?" he asked.

She chuckled softly without looking at him. "No. It just seemed to me that in a poisoning case, a lot of forensic work would be required in order to determine the culprit."

"I'll bet no one gets away with much in your geography class," he teased.

"You'd be surprised. Kids come smarter and smarter these days."

"You're right," he murmured. "Especially on the streets."

Heidi turned her head to look up at him. "Was it a lot different in New York than here?"

"No. Gangs are everywhere."

"I know. It's a tragic situation that seems to be getting worse."

He followed her into the community-ed office.

"Hi!" Carol greeted them, but her gaze rested on the man who'd just handed her the roll.

"Hi, Carol." Heidi vied for the secretary's attention. "How much do I owe for the class? Detective Poletti was kind enough to let me sign up." She opened her purse and reached for her checkbook.

"Make it out to Community School for a hundred dollars."

"That's all?"

The detective's mouth curved upward. "Didn't you

know that law-enforcement officers, like teachers, aren't in it for the money?''

"It isn't fair. Considering all the times you'll have to drive to our school, you'll end up spending most of your teaching fee on gas alone.''

It was his turn to chuckle. "I'm not worried about it, but I appreciate your concern.'' Their eyes met. Her pulse began to race when she realized that he seemed to be waiting for her.

After writing out the check, she handed it to Carol. ''Thanks. See you later.''

''Good-night,'' Carol said as they left the office and headed for the doors that led to the north parking lot.

He held one open for her. ''Where's your car?''

''Right ahead of us in the faculty parking area.''

''Before you leave, I'd like to know if you're a writer, too.''

''No. I don't have the patience.''

''Nor I. Under the circumstances, don't worry about coming up with a mystery synopsis for the class.''

Now she understood why he hadn't walked off yet. Again she'd hoped it had been for a more personal reason.

''Actually, I-I'd like to write one.'' *I need your input in Dana's case.* ''If the others think I'm working on a book, then I won't stand out. Besides, I don't want anyone to believe you're giving me preferential treatment because I missed Wednesday night or because you're using my room.''

His face broke into a smile. ''Well, then, I'll expect a masterpiece.''

She knew he was teasing her, but it was hard to think

of Dana's case in that light. "Now you've made me nervous."

Just then, several mothers she knew came out of the building and waved to her. Heidi could see the speculation in their eyes as they glanced at the handsome man standing beside her. She waved, trying to pretend she didn't know what was going through their minds.

Afraid the detective might think she was lingering because of him, she said, "It's getting late, so I'll say good-night. Thanks again for letting me join the class."

"My pleasure. See you next Wednesday."

She hurried toward her car, aware of a weakness in her legs that made her thankful she didn't have to walk far. By the time she got behind the wheel, he'd disappeared in the crowd of adults leaving the building.

Just as well she couldn't see him. It was patently ridiculous to fantasize about a man who was probably married or living with someone. Her only concern should be to get everything she could out of this class. What she learned would teach her how to start looking for hidden evidence that could lead to a reopening of Dana's case. At the very least, it should help her evaluate any private detective she might decide to hire.

But putting her new teacher out of her mind was easier said than done. By Sunday afternoon, she was still struggling to suppress thoughts of Detective Gideon Poletti as she wrote the synopsis and did the homework he'd assigned.

She was beginning to suspect he'd taken up permanent residence in her mind.

CHAPTER THREE

GIDEON TOSSED THE FRISBEE one last time, and a gust of wind blew it off course. The green plastic disc sailed over Kevin's blond head and would have disappeared into the surf if it hadn't been for Pokey.

"Good dog!" Kevin cried as the frisky beagle leaped in the air to catch it in time.

"Let's go home."

"Not yet, Dad!"

"We have to. You promised to get your homework done before I drive you back to your mom's. She made a special concession, letting you spend this weekend with me because of my birthday."

"I know. That means I won't be able to sleep over next Saturday or Sunday."

"True, but I still get you Friday night. Now you've only got one hour left. Beat you to the house!"

His ranch-style home was located two blocks from the ocean with easy access to the beach from a nearby side street.

He took off on a run. When he looked over his shoulder, Kevin wasn't far behind. Pokey kept up with him. Though the dog stayed at Gideon's, he adored Kevin and clearly rejoiced in the time they spent together.

Fay refused to have an animal in the house. No amount of pleading on Kevin's part could change her mind. But like everything else about the situation, he and his son had learned to adapt.

Between Gideon and his housekeeper, Martha, who came in every weekday afternoon for an hour to clean and prepare meals, Pokey's needs were met and he had the run of the house.

A few minutes later Kevin hauled his math book from his backpack and sat at the family-room table to start his homework. Gideon went in search of the synopses he'd brought home and joined his son. Pokey lay on the floor between them.

Kevin eyed the papers with curiosity. "What are you doing, Dad?"

"Homework. Just like you."

He laughed. "Come on."

"It's true. You're looking at the new criminology teacher for the district's adult-education program."

"Are you kidding me?"

"Nope. I have eleven students who signed up for community school." *One of them is probably the most terrific-looking female I've ever met in my life. And the most puzzling.*

"I didn't know that."

"How could you? Daniel Mcfarlane underwent emergency surgery on Friday morning and asked me to take over his class."

"What happened to him?"

"He has cancer, but I understand the operation took care of the problem. With some chemotherapy, he'll be fine."

"That's good." His son's voice trailed off. "Hey, Dad...do your students listen to you and everything?"

Gideon laughed. "So far I haven't had a problem."

"Is it fun to teach?"

"As a matter of fact, it is."

"How long are you going to be their teacher?"

"I'm not sure. Possibly till mid-May."

"That long?" Kevin cried. "When's your class?" Any change in Gideon's routine upset his son if it wasn't handled carefully.

"Wednesday and Friday nights."

Kevin's face fell. "But those are *our* nights together! Is that the reason you couldn't come and get me until late on Friday?"

"Yes. But I've been thinking about that. How would you like to come to class and watch me teach?" Gideon asked before his son could jump to the wrong conclusion. "You can get your homework done at the same time. We'll have dinner at the Jolly Roger first, and go for ice cream after."

"You'd let me come?"

"Of course."

The tears that were threatening disappeared.

"I realize this changes the way we'll spend Wednesday and Friday nights for a while. But I couldn't say no to Daniel when he asked me this favor, could I?"

"No, I guess not. Can I bring Pokey?"

"Do they let you have dogs at school?" Gideon countered.

Kevin let out a deep sigh. "No."

"I tell you what. On Wednesdays I'll get off duty early and pick you up at school. We'll go to the park or the beach and play with Pokey until we have to leave for my class. How does that sound?''

''Okay, but what about Fridays?''

''I can't get off early on Friday. But since we have the whole weekend together every other week, you can still come with me. We'll have a late dinner after class on those nights.''

''How come Daniel had to ask *you*?''

Kevin, Kevin. ''I think you already know the answer to that question.''

He lowered his head. ''Yeah. He's a good friend. I just wish Mom would let me live—''

''We've been over this ground before, son. And it's not like we won't be together. Besides, this will give you a chance to find out what I do for a living.''

''I already know,'' the boy said glumly.

Kevin was going through a stage of worrying constantly that Gideon might get killed on the job. It was one of the fears family members harbored when a parent worked in law enforcement. But Gideon had assured his fourteen-year-old that being a detective was safer than being a street cop. Still, anxiety remained.

''Do you want to hear my students' stories?'' Gideon decided a little distraction right now was more important than insisting that Kevin finish his homework. His son could do that back at Fay's.

''What stories?''

''My students are mystery writers.'' Except for one, who had an entirely different motive for attending the class. Heidi Ellis presented a mystery in her own right. One that wanted solving...

''Mystery writers?''

"That's right. They want to learn how to write what happens at the scene of a crime from a detective's point of view. I'll take them through the procedure step by step."

"That ought to be interesting."

The light had returned to his son's eyes. Thank God.

AT ELEVEN ON SUNDAY NIGHT, Heidi finished correcting her students' homework and reviewing her own and prepared for bed. While she was brushing her teeth, her phone rang.

Hoping against hope, she rinsed her mouth, then dashed into the bedroom to answer it. Caller ID was blocked.

"Hello?" she said anxiously.

"Ms. Ellis? John Cobb here."

Filled with relief, she sank onto the edge of her bed. "Thanks for calling me back. I know you've been out of town and I hate to bother you at home, but I'm desperate to help Dana. She's barely hanging on."

"I got your message earlier today and I've already made a call to her doctor and to the judge. We'll get an order to the prison so the doctor there will give her the medication she needs."

"Oh, thank you," Heidi breathed.

"Let me assure you that I'm as eager as you are for some new evidence in this case so I can take it to the district attorney."

She gripped the phone more tightly. "That's why I'm calling. I'm going to get that evidence!"

There was a brief silence on his end. "It would have to be compelling. Ron Jenke, the prosecuting attorney, has a formidable reputation for winning cases. What he presented appeared to the jury to be an airtight case. Since you and I know Dana's not guilty, that means we need a whole new approach to her case.

"Unfortunately the private detective the Turners retained after the trial never came up with anything I could use. He's given up."

"I know," Heidi murmured. "When I visited Dana last Sunday, she told me there was no hope. But I told her she was wrong and promised that the next time she saw me, I'd have something good to report." Visits to inmates had to be applied for weeks ahead. Even though Heidi knew there'd be Sundays when she couldn't go, she'd already made application for six months' worth of Sunday visits.

"Ms. Ellis, I'm sure you're aware that her case will require the best criminal investigator around. He needs to be someone who'll look at it in a completely fresh way. Someone who won't be intimidated by Jenke or persuaded by the evidence that put Dana behind bars in the first place.

"There *are* investigators like that, but it's hard to find them, let alone convince them to take a case that's already been settled."

Since the class, Gideon Poletti's image had never left her mind. "I-I've found someone who's a detective's detective. Given a little more time, I may be able to persuade him to take Dana's case."

"Good for you! I'll work with you any way I can. We'll pray for a different outcome. Dana's an innocent woman."

"She is. I won't rest until she's back home. Under

the circumstances, my parents and I would like to for-
mally retain you as our attorney to help Dana. We'll
let the Turners know what we're doing. They're so
deep in despair right now, maybe this will give them
some hope.''

"They're more fortunate than they know to have
someone like you on their side.''

"Dana and I grew up next door to each other, Mr.
Cobb. I'm an only child and I couldn't love a sister
more than I love her. As for my parents, they love her
like a daughter. No matter how long it takes, I'll fight
to get her out of prison.''

"Be assured I'll do everything in my power to help
make that happen. Call me when you're ready to
meet.''

"Thank you very much. Expect a retainer in the mail
in the next few days.''

"Let's not worry about that right now, Ms. Ellis.
Good luck. I'll look forward to hearing from you
soon.''

Heidi hung up, more convinced than ever that a man
with a reputation like Daniel Mcfarlane's would've
made sure he sent the best detective in the business to
replace him.

If Detective Poletti couldn't come up with new evidence, no one could.

But Mr. Cobb had hit on one major problem. Her
teacher was a human being with a personal life and a
career that might make it impossible for him to take
on Dana's case.

As Heidi saw it, she'd have to make him *care* about

her friend. The way to do that was to be certain her synopsis was the masterpiece he'd alluded to.

"DAD, THERE'S MAX!" Kevin started waving.

Gideon turned his head in time to see his closest friend walk through the crowded dining room of the Jolly Roger. Their friendship went back eighteen years or more. Gideon could honestly say he'd never seen Max this happy. Marriage had transformed him. The news that he was going to be a father soon kept a perpetual smile on his face.

"Hey, Kev, how's it going?" The tall, dark-haired man patted Kevin's shoulder before sitting down in the booth next to him.

"Great! Where's Gaby?"

"She had to attend a seminar after work."

"Heck," Kevin muttered.

Gideon grinned. "So, lonely old you took us up on our invitation. I guess we're better than nothing."

Max grinned back. The guy was crazy in love with his wife, Gideon mused for the thousandth time.

At twenty-two, Gideon had fallen for Fay. He'd thought she'd loved him, too. But the affair she'd had during their engagement, plus the other affair after their marriage, had destroyed that belief.

He'd had several serious relationships with women since his divorce. But something had always prevented him from proposing. It wasn't only the trust factor. Now that he'd turned thirty-seven, he realized he'd been waiting for his soul mate all along.

Someone who spoke to him, body, mind and soul.

Instantly an image of Heidi Ellis filled his head.

She'd been making an appearance there more often than not since last Friday night. Just the prospect of seeing her in a little while practically doubled his pulse rate.

"Did I tell you Gaby saw the doctor last week and we're having quadruplets?" he teased.

Gideon nodded.

"Dad! Hey, Dad—"

"What is it, son?"

Both Max and Kevin broke into laughter. Gideon looked at the two of them. "What's wrong?"

Max turned to Kevin. "How long has your dad been like this?"

"Since last Friday."

"What happened last Friday?"

"Daniel Mcfarlane had to have an operation, so he asked Dad to teach his criminology class at Mesa Junior High. That's where we're going after we eat. It's a bunch of mystery writers who signed up for adult education."

"Is that right?"

"Yeah. He read me their stories. Most of them are pretty weird."

Gideon saw the gleam in Max's eyes and knew exactly what he was thinking before he spoke.

"Mystery writers, eh? My guess is, most of them are women."

"Two are men," Kevin volunteered.

"Interesting."

"I liked the one about the mummy that was discovered in the basement of this museum in New York. But it smelled, so they unwrapped it and found a corpse.

The person had only been dead for about a week and—''

"Kevin, let's change the subject. The waitress is bringing our orders as we speak.''

While their hamburgers and shakes were being served, Max's shoulders shook in silent laughter.

"Why didn't you pick that story, Dad?" Kevin asked after taking a huge bite of his burger. "It's a lot better than the one about those call girls who poisoned the brownies.''

At this point Max let out a burst of laughter. "I think I'm going to have to come to class with you.''

By now Gideon was chuckling.

"Dad? A call girl's a prostitute, right?''

"Yeah, Dad…'' Max baited him gleefully.

"You'll learn everything you need to know in class.''

"Chicken,'' Max said under his breath.

"I'll remind you of this moment when your son or daughter starts asking questions one day.''

"I can hardly wait.'' Max was no longer joking, and the emotion in his voice said it all. The man was counting the hours until he could hold his own child in his arms. Gideon glanced at his son. Thank God for Kevin.

"So, tell me more about your students.''

"Dad says most of them are older ladies.''

Kevin's running commentary was getting Gideon into deeper water by the second.

"They're a happy, enthusiastic group of people.''

"Which one *isn't* older?'' Max asked dryly before filling his mouth with fries.

"Kevin? Would you mind telling our waitress to bring us some more water?"

"Sure."

The second he got up, Max said, "Who is she?"

"It's a moot point if she's already taken."

"But you're interested."

"Maybe."

"Maybe, hell! Is she married?"

"No."

"What's she like?"

"She's…" Gideon swallowed hard. "A candle flame in the darkness," he said softly. He didn't know where those words came from; he wasn't usually given to poetic statements. But somehow this was exactly what he meant—what he felt.

Max straightened in his chair. "Good Lord." All amusement had left his expression. "You sound like me when I first met Gabriella. Come on. I want a total description here."

"Her name is Heidi Ellis. She's a flaming redhead with blue eyes. Stands about five-two. Fantastic figure. Depending on her emotions, she's cute, beautiful, adorable, sexy and…"

"And what?"

"I don't know the rest. She's a geography teacher, not a writer. In fact, the class is being held in her room. But I know that's not the reason she was on the verge of tears when she thought I might not let her into Dan's class. I sensed all kinds of undercur—"

"The waitress said she'd be right over." Kevin interrupted, resuming his place.

Max looked at him. "Hey, Kev, what are you going to do while your dad's teaching?"

"Homework," Gideon answered for him. "He can listen while he works."

The waitress came over to refresh their water, then left the bill in front of Gideon.

"That sounds pretty good," Max said as soon as she'd left.

"I guess. But I wish Daniel had asked someone else to teach his class for him," Kevin muttered.

Invisible messages passed between Max and Gideon.

"Look at it this way, Kev. Besides the fact that he's helping out a friend, most kids don't get to see their parents at work. At least you can hear about some of the things your father has to do on the job. You'll probably learn a lot, even while you're working on your science and math. I think you're lucky."

"I know. Your dad died when you were seven."

"Both my parents died. I would've given anything to have my father around at your age. Just to be with him while he did his work would have meant a lot."

Kevin nodded. "I'm sorry they died."

Gideon could always count on Max, who was sensitive to Kevin's insecurities and knew how to talk to him.

"So am I, but it was all a long time ago." After draining his water glass, he glanced at his watch, then at Gideon. "I'll take that." He reached for the bill, but Gideon was too fast for him and grabbed it away.

"We invited you, remember? We're glad you could make it, aren't we, Kevin?"

"Heck, yeah."

"Give our love to Gaby."

Max smiled. "Don't worry." After getting to his feet, he said, "I'll see you at the office in the morning. We'll continue our conversation."

Gideon nodded to his friend in silent understanding. Concentrating on his milk shake, Kevin waved as Max walked away.

"Ready to go, Kevin?"

"Hold it. I'm almost finished."

While he gulped down the rest of his shake, Gideon's thoughts flew to the night ahead, wondering what it would bring. He could hardly wait to find out.

HEIDI DIDN'T WANT Detective Poletti to think she was being forward by arriving for class early, so she waited until the last minute before walking into the room. Everyone else was already seated.

She was disappointed to discover that their teacher was nowhere in sight. Maybe he'd had a work emergency and Mr. Johnson had opened the door for them.

As she took the only seat left, which was next to the woman named Nancy, she noticed a cute blond boy about the age of her eighth- or ninth-graders seated a few rows behind the semicircle of desks. Obviously one of the students had brought his or her son along.

He had materials and books on his desk, but his attention darted around the room as he eyed the displays.

Nancy, who looked thirtyish, turned her head toward Heidi. "Isn't this a great class?"

"Fascinating."

"To be honest," she whispered, "I'm glad the other teacher couldn't make it. This guy's gorgeous, don't you think?"

"He's very attractive, I agree."

"We've all been wondering if he's married. Do you happen to know?" she asked as the subject of their conversation suddenly walked into the room, closing the door behind him.

Tonight he was dressed in tan chinos toned with a dark-brown turtleneck and blazer—almost the color of his hair. He flashed everyone the smile Heidi had found so heart-stopping the last time the class had met.

"Good evening. What a punctual crowd! Before we get started, let me introduce my son, Kevin, who's seated behind you."

While everyone else turned around, Heidi lowered her head, fighting not to react to that unexpected revelation.

Nancy now had the answer to her question. So did Heidi.

She drew in a deep breath, acknowledging to herself that it was better to know the truth before any more time went by. With a class full of women who were open in their admiration of him, he'd probably brought his son to make the statement that he was unavailable.

"Because of the nature of my work, he can't go to the office with his dad." His comment produced chuckles. "We both thought the next best thing would be for him to sit in on this class so he can learn along with you.

"I let him read all your synopses so he'd understand what we did in class last week. For what it's worth, Lillian, he thought your mummy story was really cool."

A hand shot up.

"Yes, Jackie?"

"Lillian's the only one of us published in book-length fiction. Your son has discerning taste."

The enthusiastic group agreed with her.

Even from the distance separating them, Heidi could see the way the boy's eyes lit up.

"Did you hear that, Kevin? You picked a story that'll probably turn out to be another bestseller."

"With your help, Detective Poletti, I'm planning on it," Lillian said in obvious delight.

He flashed the class a quick smile. "In that case, let's get busy. First, I'm curious to find out how well you did your homework. After that, I'll return your synopses. We'll follow up with a five-minute break at eight. Then we'll hear a mystery scenario from Heidi before I give you your assignment for Friday."

Embarrassed, Heidi forced herself to look anywhere except at the man who held their class in thrall.

The next hour was illuminating. Just as they were all feeling pleased by his praise of their crime-scene workups, he showed the class why he was the expert.

Standing at the chalkboard, Detective Poletti proceeded to change, embellish and add to their pitiful efforts, explaining all the while. He did it with a speed and clarity that took her breath.

By the time he'd finished, the class sat there in stunned silence. He'd filled two blackboards with on-site procedures they'd never even considered, despite the textbook murder case he'd prepared for them as a guide.

"Don't bother to copy this down. While I pass back your stories, Kevin's going to give you a handout of what I put on the board so you can study it at home." He motioned to his son.

"You'll notice when you get your synopses that I've made a few suggestions for crime-scene procedures. Combined with the handout you're receiving, you ought to be able to create a credible list that'll add authenticity to your novels."

Heidi found herself wishing she had a copy of the crime-scene report that had been written the night of Amy's murder. Something told her it would pale in comparison to what she could see written on her blackboards. The detail, the number of procedures, the orderly exploration of evidence—she doubted the real crime-scene report was a fraction as thorough as this fictional one. First thing in the morning she intended to phone John Cobb's office to get what information she could.

Deep in thought, she didn't realize the boy had already started giving them the handouts. Everyone tried to engage him in conversation. Judging from his answers, he was embarrassed by all the attention. A pretty typical reaction for a boy his age.

"Thank you, Kevin."

"You're welcome."

"You must be proud of your father."

"I am."

"Are you going to be a police officer one day?"

"Maybe."

"Where'd you get your blond hair?"

"My mom."

"What grade are you in?"

"Eight."

"Where do you go to school?"

"Oakdale Middle School."

Heidi listened to the litany of questions that would

have driven any of her own students crazy, too. He wasn't a baby, but they were treating him like one. He showed remarkable poise by answering them, despite his obvious reluctance.

As he drew closer, she darted him a brief glance. He was a cute boy, but she couldn't really see any resemblance to his attractive father. Sometimes that happened.

Dana, for instance, didn't look like her parents nearly as much as Amy had. But Amy's jealousy over Dana's beauty and popularity had poisoned her soul long before someone had murdered her. That someone wasn't Dana!

When it came Heidi's turn, she thanked Kevin for the handout, remembering what he'd said about attending Oakdale Middle School. It was only a few miles from Mesa Junior High. That meant the Poletti family lived in Mission Beach.

None of it mattered of course. The fact that the detective's residence was close to Heidi's workplace should mean nothing to her.

Gideon Poletti was a professional. So if she was going to ask for his help, she needed to do it on a professional basis—and forget the way he made her heart pound.

He had a wife and child, for heaven's sake! For all she knew, there were more children at home.

Disturbed by her preoccupation with him, she opened her notebook and took out her synopsis. As he left the room with his son, she immersed herself in Dana's case. It was vital she make a compelling presentation. This was her one chance to capture the detective's interest. Since he might recognize the case, she decided she'd better use real names.

CHAPTER FOUR

AFTER THEY'D BEEN to the drinking fountain down the hall, Gideon walked Kevin back to class.

"What do you think so far?"

"It's pretty interesting. But can we please leave right at eight-thirty?"

"That's when the class is over."

"I know. But all those women are just like mom. They love to gab and they never know when to stop. Promise you won't let them?"

Gideon laughed. "It's a deal."

When they'd returned to the room, his students were back in their seats. He'd made eye contact with Heidi Ellis several times throughout the first hour, but she'd always looked away first. Such intriguing behavior had dominated his thoughts all evening.

Pleased to have reached this point in the class, he leveled his glance in her direction. Her head was lowered; she seemed to be studying her notes. Not for the first time did his breath catch at the sight of all that flaming hair splayed over her shoulders.

"Heidi? If you're ready, we'll hear from you now."

As she got up from her desk, it was hard for him to pretend dispassionate interest. Her curves were particularly appealing in the short-sleeved black sweater and tailored, gray wool pants.

She cleared her throat. "Dana Turner, twenty-five, is slowly dying in her cell. She's been imprisoned for the murder of her younger sister, Amy, nineteen, a murder Dana didn't commit. She's just learned that another detective hired by her parents after the trial has given up on her case for lack of new evidence."

The tremor in her voice alerted Gideon that this was no fabrication. Why did the name Turner ring a bell?

"Her attorney believes in her innocence, but he's told her there's nothing more he can do unless dramatic evidence should surface, warranting a new trial.

"The police incident report stated that when Amy's parents returned home from a dinner and discovered Amy's bedroom on fire, they dragged their daughter's unconscious body into the hall. She was pronounced dead by the paramedics who'd arrived soon after.

"Evidence of a physical struggle between the sisters before the fire was attested to in court. There were corresponding scratches and bruises on their bodies. Traces of Amy's hair and skin were found on a ring and under the fingernails of Dana Turner.

"Combined with her fingerprints on the gas can in the Turners' garage, this allowed the prosecuting attorney to convince the jury that Dana killed her sister in cold blood by knocking her unconscious. After Dana set her bedroom on fire, Amy was overcome by smoke inhalation and died."

Heidi paused to put the paper on the desk in front of Gideon. To the class she said, "T-that's all I have because I don't know the ending yet."

Judging by the silence in the room as she took her seat, her emotional presentation had made an impact on everyone. Their response when they did begin to comment suggested she had a winning story there.

Gideon got to his feet. "Thank you for your synopsis, Heidi."

When he said her name, her head swerved in his direction. Their eyes met, and they held that same imploring expression he'd seen last Friday. He could sense all kinds of tension coming from her.

"I'll read it and get it back to you in our next class with some comments."

"Thank you." The words were whispered.

He had to forcibly look away from her before he could gather his thoughts.

"We're going to need Emily's input before I can give you tonight's assignment. You can stay at your seat to do this, Emily. Will you describe the office where the body was found in your story? Be particular. Do it slowly so everyone can get down all the facts."

When Emily had given them a detailed picture, he said, "Good. Now that we can see the room in our minds, this is your assignment. Make as many trips through the office as necessary to come up with a list for getting forensic evidence—taking photographs, fingerprint testing and so on. I'll come up with a similar list.

"On Friday I'll ask you to share yours before I pass out a copy of mine. The writer whose list comes closest to mine will receive a prize."

A burst of approval resounded in the room, and then the bell rang.

"Let me remind you again of Daniel Mcfarlane's rule—Never assume anything."

"We won't!" most of them replied.

To his surprise he saw Heidi slip out the door. Clearly she'd decided not to stay and straighten the room. He guessed that, for some reason, she'd wanted to get away from him.

There was nothing Gideon would have liked more than to run after her, but Kevin's presence ruled out that desire.

"Let's go, Dad."

"Help me turn the desks around first."

Together they made quick work of it. Gideon grabbed his things, and once he'd turned off the lights and locked up, they were off.

"I'll turn in the attendance roll for you," Kevin said.

"Thanks. Meet me at the car."

Gideon rushed outside, hoping to talk to Heidi for a moment before she left the faculty parking lot. Unfortunately, her Audi was nowhere to be found.

Since she'd made it impossible to get an answer to the questions nagging him, he'd go to the one source who would know if the name Turner held particular significance. Daniel Mcfarlane.

After he took Kevin back to his mother's, he'd swing by Daniel's house. His mentor had come home from the hospital on Monday; according to his wife, he was feeling good and craving a report on the class.

"Dad? How come that writer didn't tell us how her mystery ended? Don't you have to know the end so you can plant clues?"

When did Kevin get so smart?

"Heidi Ellis isn't a writer," he said. "She's a geography teacher. That's her classroom we're using."

"Hmm. She's got some interesting pictures on the back wall." He turned his head in Gideon's direction. "Do you think she gets her hair dyed?"

Stifling his laughter, he said, "I don't think it's possible to manufacture that shade of red, do you?"

"I guess not. She's good-looking for a teacher."

She's good-looking, period, sport. Take it from a man who knows.

"But if she's got a son with red hair, I feel sorry for him."

"How come? You wouldn't look half bad with that color," Gideon teased.

"No, thanks!"

"So how did the homework go?"

"I finished it."

"Good for you." Gideon made a right turn and drove halfway down the street before he stopped in front of the house. "Here we are. Your mom's left the porch light on for you."

"I wish I could sleep over with you and Pokey."

"So do I." He leaned across the seat to give his boy a hug. "I'll see you on Friday at six-thirty sharp."

Kevin clung to him. "Love you, Dad."

"I love you, too, son. Have a good day tomorrow."

Saying good-night to his son was always wrenching. Gideon watched until Kevin was safely in the house, then headed for Daniel's home in Del Mar Heights.

Twenty minutes later Ellen showed him into the house. He found Daniel lying on the couch in his study watching TV. To Gideon's relief, the operation didn't seem to have set his friend back much. He hoped the chemo wouldn't be too hard on Daniel.

"Gideon! What took you so long?"

He smiled at Daniel as he sat down in the overstuffed chair next to him. "I think you're a fake. You don't look or act like someone who just got out of the hospital."

"I feel good."

"He says that now that you're here, Gideon. Can I bring you some iced tea or a cup of coffee?"

"Iced tea sounds wonderful. Thanks, Ellen."

"What about you?" she asked her husband.

"Nothing for me, honey." When she left, he said, "Tell me how the class is going."

"I have to admit I'm enjoying it more than I would've imagined. They're a smart group. So far, they've picked up on everything, and they do their homework with an enthusiasm you wouldn't believe. I guess that's what being a writer is all about."

"Good!" Daniel sighed. "I knew it was asking a lot of you to take over for me. I have to tell you I'm delighted to hear you're not ready to give up yet."

"Far from it." Heidi Ellis's emotional rendering continued to bother him. He reached into his pocket for her synopsis and handed it to Daniel.

"A new woman joined the class on Friday night. She's not really a writer, but she insisted on doing a synopsis, anyway. I want you to take a look at it."

"Would you hand me my glasses? There, on the table."

Gideon did as he asked, and while he waited for

Daniel to comment, Ellen came in with the iced tea. Gideon got to his feet to thank her, urging her to stay.

"Oh, no. I don't want to interfere. Enjoy your visit."

"I promise I won't stay long."

When she'd left the room, Gideon sat down again.

Daniel pulled off his glasses and looked up from the paper with an expression Gideon had come to recognize over the years. When his former-boss appeared to be staring at a target miles away, it meant he was onto something important.

He tapped the paper with the glasses. "This is the Turner murder case."

"So you know it? I thought the name sounded familiar. While she was reading her synopsis to the class, it had the ring of authenticity." He wouldn't forget the emotion in her voice, let alone the pleading in her eyes.

"You don't remember it?" Daniel asked in surprise. "The murder happened in the Mission Bay area. The trial must have been last August."

Gideon shook his head. "That would have been when Max and I were working on the task force to bring down the Mafia insurance-scam ring. When it was over, I took time off to spend with Kevin."

"That's right, and I'd just retired. But I remember talk around the department because it was an election year and Ron Jenke had achieved another conviction with the Turner case. He wanted the attorney general's job. Thank God he didn't get it! Between you and me, Jenke's a bastard."

"I couldn't agree more," Gideon murmured.

Daniel eyed him shrewdly. "Who's the woman, Gideon?"

"Heidi Ellis. Does her name sound familiar?" He hoped it didn't.

"No."

Relieved, he said, "She teaches geography at Mesa Junior High. It was her blackboard you wrote on. That's how she found out about the night class."

Daniel nodded slowly but didn't respond. Growing anxious, Gideon reached for his tea and drained the glass.

"If she's not a writer," Daniel finally said, "I suppose it's possible she chose a real murder case from the San Diego area just to make it easier to do the assignment, but—"

"But you don't buy that theory," Gideon finished for him. "Neither do I. Since she missed the first class and wasn't one of the aspiring mystery writers, I told her she didn't have to do a synopsis, but she insisted. Her reasons for wanting to do it were plausible enough. But they didn't match the intensity of her emotions."

Daniel stared at Gideon. "She could be a close relative or friend who hasn't been able to reconcile Dana Turner's imprisonment. Or she—"

"Don't say it!" Unable to remain seated, Gideon jumped to his feet and began pacing. He felt the older man's eyes on him.

"It sounds like you have a personal interest in this woman."

"Maybe."

"There's no maybe about it."

"Hell, Dan…"

He knew what his mentor was thinking. It was the same thing Gideon had been thinking on the drive over.

When you worked in homicide, you dealt with profiles and statistics. More often than not, it had been proved that a person who came out of the woodwork after a settled murder case either knew something about it that hadn't come to light or was an accessory to the crime. In some instances these people turned out to be the real killers. *Lord.*

"Tell Rodman you want to take a look at the case. Call me when you've learned anything."

Grim-faced, Gideon nodded. "Thanks. Now I'd better leave before Ellen pushes me out the door. Take care of yourself. We all want you around for a long time."

"I'm planning on it. Here." He returned Heidi's assignment, then gave him a penetrating look. "In all the time we've been friends and colleagues, I've never known you to lose your objectivity. This woman must be exceptional. A word of advice?"

"What's that?" Gideon muttered.

"I'm surprised you have to ask. Rule number one of course."

Suitably chastened, he gave Daniel's shoulder a squeeze, then let himself out of the house.

All the way home he repeated the words in his head. *Never assume anything.* But by the time he pulled to his driveway, nothing about the situation was any clearer.

She was the first woman in years for whom he'd felt

this kind of attraction, and she had problems he'd only begun to grasp. How had it happened?

Max would be able to relate to his dilemma. He'd fallen for Gaby when he'd believed her to be his enemy. The guy had gone through hell before he'd learned the truth.

Fortunately for Max, the car crash that had brought the two of them together really *had* been an accident— not part of the insurance scam—whereas Heidi Ellis's interest in the criminology class was anything but accidental.

Thanks to Daniel, Gideon might have a chance to check out this case and have some answers before Friday night's class. Until he determined otherwise, he was going to operate on the premise that Heidi was a grieving friend or relative of Dana Turner's.

He *had* to believe that because he had every intention of getting to know her much better....

As soon as school let out on Friday afternoon, Heidi drove to her parents' house to discuss her conversation with Mr. Cobb. Over dinner, she explained why she was taking the night class. Her parents thought approaching Detective Poletti was a wonderful idea.

When she left for school, she could hardly wait to hear his comments on her synopsis. But she wanted to talk to him about Dana when no one else was around.

He might bring his son to class again, and in that case the two of them would probably leave the minute it was over. If she hoped to have a private talk with him, her best bet would be to get there ahead of everyone else.

Depending on his reaction to the news that her story was a real murder case, she'd try to discover whether he ever did investigative work on the side. With her parents' help, she was prepared to meet any price he named.

Pleased to see that her door was already open, she steeled herself not to think about him in any way but as a detective who might be willing to look into Dana's case.

At first she thought no one was inside. Then she spotted his son at the back of the room, looking at the photographs she'd had enlarged for her display.

He must have heard her because he turned around. "Hi!"

"Hi, yourself!" She put her purse on the closest chair, then walked toward him. "Where's your father?"

"In the office making copies of your assignment for next week. That's you in the big picture, isn't it?" He pointed to it.

"A much younger me, yes." She smiled. "I'm surprised you could pick me out among all the other people in our group."

"That was easy. None of them has red hair. How come you went to Africa?"

He had sharp eyes. In the picture her hair was swept back and she wore a hat that covered most of it.

"After my best friend and I graduated from high

school, we took a trip around the world. There she is, standing between those two Africans.''

His warm brown eyes widened. ''You and your friend went around the world?''

''Yes. It isn't as impossible as it sounds. We got a really good deal with an airline. If you keep flying west until you get back home again, it doesn't cost as much. We made as many stops as we could fit in. Our favorite place was Kenya.''

''Did you go on safari?''

''Yes. We saw everything from gazelles and zebras to hippos playing in the river. It was fabulous.''

''What was your favorite?''

''The baby giraffes. They're so cute the way they stay close to their mothers. See this photograph?'' She pointed to one in the corner. ''I snapped this picture when the guide took us on horseback up a mountain.

''It was all misty. Then suddenly we were above it and discovered we'd met up with a whole herd of mother giraffes feeding on tree leaves with their young. We passed through them without creating a disturbance. I was able to get close to one of the babies.''

''You were lucky.''

''I was. My guide had been taking people to that spot for years, so the giraffes weren't frightened. Do you love animals?''

''Yeah.''

''Do you have a pet?''

He nodded with a smile. ''A beagle. His name is Pokey.''

''Does that mean he's slow?''

"No. Dad called him that because he pokes his nose into everyone's business."

"Kind of sounds like your father."

His smile faded. "What do you mean?"

"Detectives poke around looking for evidence. The bad guys don't like it."

"Oh…yeah."

One thing she'd found out in a big hurry. This boy was very protective of his father.

"How would you like to see some of the animals I took pictures of? I've got them on disks so you can view them on the computer."

"That would be great!"

"Then come on over here. I'll turn it on so you can get started. I also have a disk with pictures of the apes in the Jane Goodall preserve."

A minute later, Kevin was completely absorbed by the photographs.

She stood up and turned to walk to the front, then let out a soft gasp. Not two feet away stood her teacher. He was wearing a light-gray suit tonight with a charcoal shirt. There was no way she could be indifferent to him, not when he was the most attractive man she'd ever met in her life.

"Detective Poletti—how long have you been here?"

His gaze made a flattering sweep of her body, sending her heart slamming into her ribs. "Long enough to be disappointed that there's no picture of you mingling with the giraffes."

Heat streamed into her cheeks as she realized he'd overheard a great deal.

"Dad! You should see all her pictures! They're just like *National Geographic*'s. How about us going to Kenya, instead of Alaska this summer?"

His father put his hands on his hips in a totally masculine stance. "I might've known I couldn't leave my son alone in your fascinating classroom for two minutes. Now I'll never hear the end of it."

Before she took another breath—if she could even catch it—she needed to find out one crucial piece of information. "Have you and your wife taken Kevin to Alaska before?"

There was a long pause. "My ex-wife remarried years ago," he said in a flat voice. "But to answer your question, Kevin and I spend a few weeks every summer fishing near Anchorage."

Delight spread through her. She reminded herself that she'd only spent two class sessions with him and that her reaction was out of proportion to what it should have been. The reminder didn't help.

Fearing the detective could tell what was going on inside her, she turned in his son's direction. "You're a fortunate guy, Kevin. That's something I've never done."

He was staring at the screen as he spoke. "It's a lot of fun. We fly to this island in a pontoon plane."

"Is it scary?"

"Probably as scary as one of those two-seater bush planes flying you to your camp in Kenya," his father said. "Come on up to the desk and I'll give you back your assignment."

She followed him to the front, conscious of his presence, his powerful physique. Now that she knew he wasn't married, she refused to feel guilty at the enjoyment she derived from just looking at him. Only time would tell if some other woman held his heart. Of course, that meant she'd have to be lucky enough to be given the chance to find out.

As he returned her paper, three of the writers came into the room. Her opportunity for a private conversation was gone. Maybe after class tonight, she could make an appointment to talk to him before the next session.

"Thank you for allowing me to hand it in."

"You're welcome."

Once in her seat, she started reading the comments he'd made below her synopsis:

Heidi—since you're not a writer, I find myself wondering why you chose to write a synopsis of the Mission Bay murder case, which was settled last August. I must confess I'd be interested to hear your answer. If it's all right with you, I'll phone you this weekend and set up a time we can meet outside of class.

WHILE HE GREETED everyone, Gideon watched Heidi Ellis to gauge her reaction to his note. One second her head was bent in concentration. The next it came up sharply, shifting the cloud of red-gold around her shoulders.

Their eyes clung as she nodded in silent agreement.

He was pleased with her response—no, *pleased* wasn't the word. *Excited* was a better one to explain how he felt, because he'd be seeing her again soon— on Saturday he hoped. If she was in love with someone else, he'd face that problem when he had to.

In much better spirits than when he'd arrived, he put his students to work writing their list of crime-scene procedures on the board. The eager group became so involved he dispensed with the break and worked them straight through. A few minutes before the bell, he announced the winner.

''Natalie's list has only one item fewer than mine. Congratulations.''

As everyone clapped, Gideon handed her a wrapped package. ''It's a pocket-size book called *The Layman's Guide to the World of Crime-Scene Forensics.* Let's hope it helps you in writing many famous mysteries one day.''

Another grandmotherly type, she gave him a quick hug before everyone crowded around, anxious to see it. Gratified that the gift seemed to be such a hit, he decided to give out a prize every week.

Amid the commotion, he signaled Kevin to pass out their assignments for Wednesday.

''You'll need the coroner's report from your packet to fill out this sheet,'' he said, speaking above the din. ''When you come next week, I'll have a coroner here who'll discuss the case of the poisoned woman and answer your questions.''

More murmurs of approval met his announcement.

Half-a-dozen writers stopped by the desk to tell him this was the most exciting class they'd ever taken.

When the room had emptied, Heidi was still there, straightening the desks. A smile hovered at the corners of her mouth. "High praise, Detective. I think I'm jealous. After six years of teaching, I can count on one hand the number of kids who paid me such effusive compliments."

"Come on, Dad. Let's go! You promised," Kevin said.

For the first time in years, Gideon was torn between pleasing his son and giving in to his own desires.

"Go with him," she urged in a quiet aside. "I'll lock up."

The last thing Gideon wanted to do was leave. "You'll be hearing from me tomorrow."

"I'll be home."

He nodded, and their eyes met one last time.

Kevin was halfway out the door before Gideon caught up with him. "I think you've forgotten to tell her something important," he told his son.

Kevin turned to her. "Thanks for letting me use your computer, Ms. Ellis. Those were great pictures."

"I'm glad you enjoyed them. Next time if you have homework that has to be done on the computer, feel free to use mine."

"Thanks."

"You're welcome. Have fun with Pokey."

Gideon caught the private smile they gave each other. "What was that all about?" he asked when they reached the hallway.

"Ms. Ellis said you were like our dog because you poke around looking for evidence."

Pleased to hear she'd been talking about him, Gideon chuckled. "What else did you two discuss?"

"She's been around the world."

In a short period of time, Kevin had found out quite a lot. "That's pretty amazing."

"How much do you think it costs?"

"A lot more than we spend vacationing in Alaska."

"I thought schoolteachers were poor."

"They make enough to live." He had yet to learn anything about Heidi Ellis's background.

As for taking a look at the Turner case, that would have to wait until Monday. Both yesterday and today, he'd had to work on a new murder investigation. His responsibilities had made it impossible to get into the archives.

Under the circumstances, maybe it was just as well he didn't have a lot of preconceived notions about the case—or her. Something had happened to him when she'd walked into that class a week ago. Something almost overwhelming...

Maybe he was getting ahead of himself here. But if the same thing was happening to her, he didn't want anything to spoil what might happen between them.

"Dad? Could you give me an advance on my allowance?"

Gideon darted his son a glance as they pulled into the mainstream of traffic. "How come?"

"It's Brad's birthday tomorrow. I want to get him a CD for his PlayStation."

"No problem."

"Thanks."

"What does he have planned?"

"I think a bunch of us are going to a movie. Then his parents are taking us to dinner somewhere. I don't know for sure."

"That sounds like fun."

"Yeah. What are *you* going to do?"

I'd like to know the answer to that myself. "I'll probably put in a day's work." And in the evening? That all depended on a certain redhead. Gideon was counting the hours until he saw her again.

CHAPTER FIVE

SHE WAS IN THE MIDDLE of scouring the bathroom when the phone rang. Heidi dashed into her bedroom to answer it, noting that it was almost noon. Waiting for Detective Poletti to call had filled her with so much nervous excitement she'd done a more thorough job of her Saturday housecleaning than usual.

The caller ID indicated the person's number had been blocked. She grabbed the receiver, hoping it wasn't someone else telling her she'd won a so-called prize—a free cruise to the Bahamas or a month's subscription to the *Wall Street Journal* or something. There'd been three of those already this morning.

"Hello?" She knew she sounded out of breath.

"Heidi?" His voice was deep, vibrant. She sank onto the bed she'd just made. "It's Gideon Poletti."

"Good morning." The thrill of talking to him had left her tongue-tied.

"Did I catch you at a bad time?"

"Not at all. I've been cleaning. I needed a break, anyway."

"I needed one, too. I've been working on a complicated case all morning. What's your schedule like for this weekend? Would Saturday or Sunday night be better for you to go out to dinner?"

Her hand tightened on the receiver. "Tonight, if that's all right." Depending on the outcome of their conversation, Heidi planned to visit Dana tomorrow. It was an all-day trip. She never got back before dark.

"Good. That works out well for me, too. Can you be ready by five? There's a new Mexican restaurant in the Oakdale Plaza I've been meaning to try out. They don't take reservations, but I figure if we get there early, we won't have to stand in line too long. I confess I could eat Mexican food every night and never get tired of it."

"I love it, too. That sounds wonderful. I'll be ready."

"What's your address?"

"I live in a fourplex apartment building at 422 Brierwood Avenue in Mission Beach. It's only three blocks from Mesa Junior High. Apartment C. It's upstairs on the right."

"I'll find you." She heard the click.

She trembled a little at his choice of words just now. *I'll find you.* He'd made it sound personal, the way he'd spoken in that intimate tone.

Then she scoffed at herself. She was so attracted to him she was reading too much into their brief conversation.

She had to be cautious, not overreact. What if she'd misunderstood the reason for his invitation? He was a professional. No doubt he'd chosen an early dinner as a way of letting her know he'd asked her out purely to learn why she'd used the Turner murder case for her class assignment.

It was possible that nothing more than discretion and

a detective's instinctive curiosity had motivated him to talk to her privately, away from the other writers in the class.

Forcing herself to keep those thoughts foremost in her mind, she finished her housecleaning, then ran errands for a couple of hours. Around three, she returned to wash her hair and get ready.

She must have changed outfits five times, finally settling on a navy gabardine coat dress with gold braid and buttons down the front. It looked smart, not too dressy and would keep her comfortable in the brisk evening air.

At exactly five the doorbell rang. Not wanting to appear too eager, she waited a moment before answering. The second she opened the door, she felt the impact of those brilliant blue eyes taking in every part of her, from her navy high heels to the last strand of hair on her head.

There was instant stillness between them as her gaze traveled over him. He wore a dressy black polo shirt and tan chinos. It was rude to stare, but she couldn't help herself.

"Y-you're right on time," she stammered.

"I've been told it's one of my worst faults."

Heidi smiled. "Hardly."

"Don't worry if you're not ready yet."

"I am. Let me grab my purse and we'll go."

She left the door open while she hurried over to the couch where she'd put her purse. Once she'd rejoined him, she locked the door, then started down the steps. He caught up with her at the bottom and clasped her elbow to guide her out to the curb, where he'd parked his Acura. As he opened the car door, he suddenly said, "By the way, you look stunning in that dress."

Her heart went crazy. "Thank you."

She wanted to tell him he always looked wonderful, but she didn't dare. It was too soon.

Although she couldn't deny there was a candid look of appreciation in his eyes, he probably made every woman he met feel beautiful. The female writers in the class, regardless of age, were totally charmed by him. Some men had that ability.

Still physically aware of him, she needed something to do with her hands and reached over to fasten the seat belt.

"You smell good, too," he added before moving his car into traffic.

She wasn't used to being with a man who felt so at ease in giving a compliment. Jeff had been an entirely different kind of person.

"It must be my shampoo."

"Strawberries and red hair make a perfect combination. Did you inherit that color from your mother or your father?"

"My mom."

"How many of your brothers and sisters are so endowed?"

"I'm an only child," she told him. "What about you?"

"I have an older married sister with three children, plus my parents. They all live in New York. Kevin and I get out to see them every summer. This coming Thanksgiving, it's my turn to have my son with me, so my family's flying here to spend the holiday with us."

Visitation. Half the kids in her classes had to cope with it, their lives split between two parents, two homes and sometimes two separate agendas.

"I'm sure Kevin will enjoy that," she said. "He's a wonderful boy."

Gideon flashed her a sidelong glance. "I think so, too."

"He idolizes you."

"I feel like that about my parents, as well. How about you?"

She smiled at him. "The same. Fortunately for me they only live ten minutes away. I can drop in on them whenever I don't feel like behaving as an adult."

That comment made him laugh. She loved the sound of a man's uninhibited laughter.

She'd been so involved in their conversation, she didn't realize they'd already arrived at the crowded Oakdale Plaza parking lot. There wasn't a free space in sight. Late Saturday afternoon was the worst.

As she started to suggest they go somewhere else, a car backed out of a spot just in front of them and drove off.

"How come that never happens to me?" she lamented as Gideon pulled into the space.

He glanced at her, a gleam in his eyes. "Stick with me and you'll find out."

It was her turn to laugh gently. "I'll remember that."

"Good," he whispered.

They might have been a few feet apart, but she felt his warmth and energy as though they were in each other's arms.

So far he hadn't broached the subject that had prompted this outing. Did he always treat women so...so *gallantly,* even on police business?

Or could she be forgiven for thinking he really might have an interest in her beyond the synopsis she'd written? She felt as if her life hinged on the answer to that question.

Afraid to want something she might not be able to have, she struggled to keep her emotions under control.

He got out of the car and came around to her door. "There's no line outside the restaurant. I believe we're in luck."

His comments jerked her back to the present. "Let's hurry and get a table before the swarm descends."

Heidi admitted to many human flaws, but feeling superior around other people had never been one of them. Until now. As he ushered her into the restaurant, the envy coming from a lot of the women there was almost tangible.

She couldn't blame them. Being escorted by a rugged-looking man of Detective Poletti's physical stature and grace bordered on the realm of her own fantasies, too. But there was one difference. This was no dream.

He gave his name to the hostess, then put a protective hand on her back as they joined the small line waiting to be seated. All of Heidi's concentration focused on the feel of his hand, the slight pressure, the heat of his skin through her dress.

The newest restaurant in the area had done a nice job of creating a Mexican-patio feel throughout, with plenty of trees, colorful tiled tables and wrought-iron chairs. She could hear mariachi music—*loud* mariachi music.

He lowered his head to talk to her. "Would you like to have a drink in the bar until they call our table?"

She'd felt his smooth-shaven jaw brush her temple. The clean scent of the soap he'd used clung to his skin. Though the contact was minimal, it sent a feathery shiver of delight down her spine, making it difficult for her to think with any coherence.

"I'd love it," she managed.

"So would I," he whispered into her hair. Her bones turned to liquid and she was doubly glad of his hand on her back. It seemed to anchor her, somehow.

He signaled to the hostess where they'd be, then urged Heidi forward past a roomful of diners to the bar. This time his arm was firmly around her waist.

"Dad!" a boy's voice cried above the cacophony of sounds and music.

Physically connected to Gideon, she felt his body immediately tauten. He murmured his son's name, then whirled her around with him in time to see Kevin get up from a table, surrounded by other teenage boys. He dodged the balloons and came running toward his father.

"What are you doing here?" The question bordered on accusation.

"Having dinner, just like you," his father answered in a voice of enviable calm. "How about saying hello to Ms. Ellis?"

Kevin's eyes sent her a withering glance. "Hello." Gone was all the friendliness of last evening.

"Hi, Kevin. It looks like a birthday party."

"Yeah." The one word came out stiffly, a reluctant whisper. He gazed up at his father once more. His eyes were suspiciously bright.

Heidi didn't have to be a mind reader to understand what Kevin was feeling. It was all right for her to be part of his dad's night class. But seeing her here with his father's arm around her must have been a genuine shock.

Surely Gideon knew that, but his arm remained in place. If anything, it tightened. Something was going on that she didn't understand. The last thing she wanted was to create problems between the two of them.

She knew Gideon would tell her about it later, but Heidi was troubled by his son's pain. There was too much pain in the world. In fact, she was meeting with Gideon tonight in an attempt to end the pain her friend and their families were suffering if she could.

"Poletti? Poletti?"

He glanced at his son. "Our table's being called. We have to go. I'll call you later tonight and you can tell me about the party."

The boy's face paled. Heidi couldn't bear it.

"Kevin?" She broke the awkward silence. "Have you had the birthday cake yet?"

His eyes were mere slits when he finally deigned to look at her. "Yeah."

"Then your friend probably won't mind if you sit at our table."

A tremor rocked Gideon's body, one she could feel to her fingertips. He hadn't liked her suggestion.

Maybe she *had* spoken out of turn. It was probably because she taught children that age; she knew how vulnerable they were. The nurturer in her refused to stay silent.

"No, thank you."

She kept hoping Gideon would urge his son to join them. Instead, he said, "Looks like your friends are waiting for you, Kevin. See you later."

He moved his hand to Heidi's shoulder. "Let's find out where we're seated."

They worked their way to the front of the restaurant again, but Heidi knew she wouldn't be able to swallow a bite of food. Her appetite, along with her excitement, had fled.

She turned to him before he could approach the hostess. "Detective Poletti?"

The tension between them was explosive.

He grimaced. "My name is Gideon. I'd like to hear you use it."

"All right." She fought for breath. "Gideon. If you don't mind, I'd feel more comfortable if we left the restaurant. We can eat anywhere else you want. Just not here. Please."

She started out the entrance ahead of him.

HELL.

Those gorgeous blue eyes were pleading with him again.

She'd read the incident with his son correctly. In her own way, she seemed to be as vulnerable as Kevin.

Hell and damnation.

He put the key in the ignition. "Obviously you're not hungry right now. How would you feel about going to my house in Ocean Beach? By the time we get there, maybe your appetite will have returned.''

She bit the soft underside of her lip. ''What if Ke—''

''If you're worried about that, he lives with his mother and stepfather,'' Gideon interrupted her. ''She'll be expecting him home right after the party. You and I have some talking to do—in private.''

''Nevertheless, I think it might be better if we went back to my apartment. We can order pizza, if you'd like.''

''I'd like.''

Relieved that she'd offered a compromise, one that meant they'd be spending the rest of the evening together, he started the engine. They drove to her apartment in silence. She didn't seem inclined to talk. It didn't matter. He needed time to gather his thoughts.

Meeting her had already changed his life. He knew it from the way he'd felt when he'd gotten out of bed this morning. A heightened sense of well-being. An awareness of new possibilities.

Suddenly he found himself contemplating a future he hadn't even dared to dream about since his early twenties, when he was a rookie cop in New York. He had no intention of losing Heidi Ellis at the starting line.

A few minutes later, he was following her into the apartment. He'd only caught a glimpse of the interior earlier.

Now he looked all around, taking in the white walls, framed photographs and Impressionist prints. She had dozens of interesting books on art and literature in a tall narrow walnut case that went to the ceiling. An Italian credenza rested against one wall.

Two matching striped French-provincial chairs flanked a large square glass coffee table. In the center was a copper pot filled with shocking-pink azaleas. Other trees and plants were placed in corners and niches.

A comfortable-looking dark-red sofa with a pile of colorful pillows dominated the other wall. Hardwood floors were covered by an Oriental rug with a small floral design that tied all the colors of the room together.

If she wasn't a schoolteacher, he bet she could make her living as an interior decorator. The furnishings in her classroom were an extension of what he could see here.

"I feel like I've walked into a trendy New York loft on the upper west side."

She looked pleased by the comment. "No one's ever told me that before. But then, I've never known a native New Yorker."

"I'm a Southern Californian by now."

"You still have a slight accent. Don't ever lose it."

They were dancing around each other, beginning the ritual of getting to know each other. It wasn't just the words. They were communicating on so many levels Gideon felt an exhilaration he could scarcely contain.

"What do you like on your pizza?" she asked.

"Everything but anchovies."

"I'll phone from the kitchen. Can I bring you some coffee or a cola?"

"Cola sounds good."

She nodded. "I'll be right back."

After she'd disappeared, he walked to the coffee table and picked up an oversize book comparing the pyramids of Egypt and Mesoamerica. Intrigued, he sat on the couch to thumb through it.

When she returned and set his drink on the table, he glanced up. "Have you traveled to both places?"

"Yes. I went inside the pyramid you're looking at right now."

"That must have been an incredible experience."

"It was—in more ways than one." She sat at the other end of the couch, holding her drink. "I almost died of the heat. It was 135 degrees in the tunnel, and the odor was horrendous. Part of the time, you had to bend way down while you walked. In some spots a man your size would've been forced to get down on his hands and knees."

His lips twitched. "I would never have guessed."

"Me, neither," she said in a wry voice. "I'm afraid that when we reached the inner chambers of the tomb, our guide's explanation washed right over me because I was weaving in and out of consciousness from lack of air. I bought this book so I could see what I'd missed, but I don't admit that to my students."

Everything she said and did charmed him.

He closed the cover and sat back against the pillows with his drink. "What about the New World pyramids?" he asked.

"You climb them on the outside in 130-degree heat and suffer vertigo before you reach the top. Choose your poison."

The word reminded them both of the class assignment. She returned his smile.

He finished his drink and put the glass back on the table. "Heidi...I want to apologize for my son's behavior."

She shook her head. "It's not necessary."

"I think it is." He sat forward. "Because of my career, Kevin's always worried that something might happen to me. I've taken him to therapy to help him overcome his fear.

"Now that he's older, he's doing a lot better in that department. However, after tonight's demonstration, it's obvious he's developed another problem."

"You mean he hasn't had trouble sharing you before now?"

"No. I haven't remarried, but I've had several relationships with women over the years. He accepted their presence in my life. You have to understand that his rudeness to you came as a tremendous shock to me. I've never seen that kind of behavior from him before."

"Did he have any idea of your plans for this evening?"

"No."

"Then I can see why he was upset. It was one thing to watch you interact with me in class. But quite another to—"

"To discover me escorting you in public," he broke in.

She avoided his eyes and took another sip of her drink. "I have no doubt that when you explain the reason you took me to dinner, he'll be reassured."

Gideon shook his head. "What if I want to take you out to dinner tomorrow night?" he asked quietly. "And the night after that?"

MORE THAN ANYTHING in the world, Heidi had hoped to hear those words from him. She just hadn't expected such candor tonight. Yet she shouldn't have been surprised. Gideon's inquiring nature compelled him to drive unrelentingly until he found the answer he sought. It was professional curiosity, she told herself yet again. Nothing personal.

"If I'm moving too fast for you, I won't apologize," he murmured. "I know in my gut you're not indifferent to me. That's why Kevin fell apart tonight. He sensed the chemistry between us and feels threatened by it."

She jumped up from the couch. "Your son adores you. Much as I might enjoy your company, he has a prior claim. I think it would be better if we only saw each other during class."

"Unless this is your way of telling me you're involved with someone else, I refuse to accept that."

His blunt honesty was as shocking as it was thrilling. With a few succinct words he'd established ground rules that required she be equally candid. He wouldn't accept anything less.

"Th-there's no one else, but—"

"But nothing," he cut in with almost forbidding finality. "That's all I needed to know. Kevin's going to have to come to grips with the fact that his father has a personal life—"

A knock on the door interrupted them.

"I'll get it." With effortless agility he intercepted

her and paid the delivery man for the pizza. "Where do you want us to eat?"

"In the dining area. We'll be more comfortable there. I've made a salad, as well."

He followed her through the living room to a roomy white-and-yellow alcove with a bay window, where she'd hung two large baskets of flowering plants. The square oak pedestal table stood near a matching hutch, complete with hand-painted pottery. The room's warm sunny feel delighted him.

"You have superb taste," he said when they'd settled down to enjoy their pizza and salad.

"I can't take any credit. My mother's family has dealt in furniture and antiques since the early 1900s. One of the perks of being her daughter was that my best friend and I started working at the warehouse from the age of fourteen.

"When something came in that we felt we couldn't live without, we worked all the overtime they'd give us to pay for it. If you think my apartment's interesting, you should have seen Dana's...before she was sent to prison."

There. She'd been waiting for the right opening. Now it was out.

Gideon flashed her a lightning glance, then put down his half-eaten piece of pizza.

"She didn't kill Amy!" Heidi blurted. Tears sprang to her eyes. "Her family lives next door to mine. We grew up like sisters. I know her as well as I know myself. She's *dying* in that prison, Gideon." Her voice trembled. "I've got to get her out of there or my life's not going to be worth living, either!"

"Lord," she heard him whisper.

"When I found out that the retired head of San Diego's Homicide division was teaching a criminology class in my room, I considered it a godsend. That's why—"

"You don't need to explain," he interjected.

"You'll never know how grateful I am that you let me join the class. Already I've learned so much, and I *know* vital evidence was overlooked in her case. The other night I phoned John Cobb, Dana's attorney."

"He's one of the best around."

She sucked in her breath. "I hope you're right, Gideon. He believes in Dana's innocence, but he said that unless we come up with compelling new evidence, he won't be able to get the case reopened."

"That's because he knows how difficult it is to do that."

"But surely it's not impossible...."

He reached out to squeeze her hand. Warmth spread through her body. "No. Nothing's impossible if you want it badly enough."

"I want it for her parents, too. It's so awful, Gideon. They spend their days between visiting the prison and the cemetery where Amy's buried."

With her pulse pounding in her ears, she said, "Do you thi—"

Once again they were interrupted, this time by Gideon's cell phone. Frowning, he let go of her hand and pulled the phone from his trouser pocket.

Not wanting to appear too curious, she started clearing the table. It sounded as though he was trying to appease someone. Heidi had an idea who that someone was.

Judging by Gideon's sober expression when he put his phone away, she was expecting the worst. He didn't disappoint her. "That was Kevin," he said. "He was sobbing so hard I could hardly understand him."

Heartsick, she rested her hip against the counter. "I'm not surprised."

He shook his head, frowning. "Frankly, I *am*. Do you know that boy left the restaurant, caught the bus to my house, let himself in, and has been waiting for me?"

"Like he's the parent?" she teased, trying to lighten his burden.

"Exactly. But he crossed a line tonight. To make matters worse, his mother has no idea he's not with Brad. He swore his friend to secrecy, but secrets have a way of getting out. If she hears what happened, she'll punish him by curtailing his visits with me for a while."

"Can she ignore his visitation rights?"

His eyes met hers. "No. The judge would tell her she'd have to discipline him another way, but I don't want to give her the opportunity to make trouble. I'm afraid I've got to go. The sooner I get Kevin home, the better."

"I agree."

She didn't want him to go, but it couldn't be helped. His son needed him, needed his reassurance.

"I'll call you tonight, no matter how late it is."

She nodded, feeling his reluctance to leave. He wheeled around abruptly and left her apartment.

After she heard the front door close, she hurried into the living room, toward the shuttered window, and peered out through the slats. As she watched him dash toward his car, she couldn't stop her heart from chasing after him.

"ARE YOU MAD at me?"

Gideon gripped the steering wheel a little more tightly as he backed the car out of the driveway and headed for Mission Beach. "No. I'm angry at myself."

Kevin's head jerked toward him in surprise. "How come?"

"I broke a rule I learned from Daniel."

"What rule?"

"Never assume anything."

"I don't get it."

He drew in a deep breath. "It doesn't matter. The important thing is that over the last couple of years you've changed from a boy into a teenager. It happened without my really being aware of it...until tonight. Long ago I should've had the talk I'm going to have with you now. It would've prevented what happened at the restaurant earlier this evening."

His son lowered his head without saying anything.

"I'm a man who believes that if you're in love with a woman, you don't live with her the way a lot of men do. You *marry* her.

"Over the years I've had a series of relationships with women, but when it came right down to it, I realized I wasn't in love with any of them. That's why I've been single all this time. It's the reason you've never questioned my living alone.

"Where I made my mistake was not telling you that I've always wanted to get married again, provided I meet the right woman."

"But that would ruin everything!" Kevin exploded.

Something twisted unpleasantly in Gideon's stomach. He could see this was going to take time. Above all, he needed wisdom and patience to help his son understand it wasn't the end of life as he knew it.

"Kevin, you know I love you more than anything in the world."

After a long silence, the boy muttered, "I *thought* you did."

Gideon recognized that it was his son's anger talking. He'd always had to compete with his stepfather for his mother's love.

"You're in love with *her,* aren't you!" he accused unexpectedly. "All the guys saw your arm around her."

Dear God. More damage had been done than he'd realized.

"Let's just say I'm very attracted to Heidi. However, no one knows what the future holds. I'm planning to spend more time with her to explore what might be between us. But whatever happens, nothing's going to change my relationship with you. It couldn't. That's because you're my son and we're a team. We always will be."

Kevin didn't say another word the rest of the way home. When they pulled up to the curb in front of Fay's house, he got out of the car without giving Gideon a hug. That was a first.

It hurt like hell.

When Kevin turned to shut the door, his eyes glittered with a combination of anger and pain. "I thought I was going to live with you when I turned eighteen, but I won't if you marry *her*. I hate her, and I don't want to go to your class anymore."

Long after he'd run into the house, Gideon sat there in pained disbelief as his son's words reverberated in his head.

IT WAS TEN AFTER ELEVEN when Heidi finished correcting the last test to hand back to her students on Monday. She was grateful for something to do—something to distract her so she wouldn't go crazy waiting for the phone to ring.

Though Gideon had told her he'd call later tonight, she wasn't really counting on it. His son was upset. No telling how long it would take to calm his fears.

Her experience as a teacher had shown her how unpredictable the early teenage years could be when hormones were raging and problems could no longer be solved with a hug from Mom followed by a batch of her homemade cookies.

She turned off the TV, which had provided background noise, and got ready for bed. No sooner had her head touched the pillow than the phone rang.

Sitting up, she reached for the receiver. "Hello?"

"Heidi? It's Gideon."

She willed her heart to slow down. "How did it go? Is he feeling better now?"

"I'm afraid not."

The bleakness in his voice worried her. "I'm so sorry."

"So am I. But I don't want to talk about that right now. What are you doing tomorrow?"

She swallowed hard. "I had plans to visit Dana."

"Why don't I pick you up and we'll go together?"

"You mean it?" she cried. Meeting Gideon would breathe new life into her friend, she was sure of it.

"I was going to look at her case on Monday, but I'd prefer to talk to her first and form my own impressions without any bias."

A sob escaped her throat. "You don't know...you can't imagine what this will do for her." Heidi couldn't prevent her emotions from spilling over.

"I'll be by at ten. We can stop for lunch on the way."

"Thank you," she whispered. "Thank you."

You have no idea what this means to me.

CHAPTER SIX

THE RINGING OF A PHONE seemed to be part of Gideon's jumbled dream. But when the sound went on and on, he realized it couldn't be. Half-awake, he reached for the phone at the side of his bed. "Poletti here."

"How come you didn't tell me Kevin rode the bus clear out to your house after the birthday party last evening?"

Fay.

According to Gideon's watch, it was only five-thirty in the morning. He jackknifed into a sitting position. "What's wrong?"

"We're at St. Anne's emergency room. Kevin woke up with a bad pain in his stomach, but the doctor couldn't find anything wrong with him. It really angered me when he suggested my son was having psychological problems and ought to get counseling. We've been there and done that."

Gideon's eyes closed tightly.

"They gave him a mild sedative. It seemed to calm him a little. That's when it all came out—about seeing you at the restaurant with some redhead you couldn't keep your hands off. Why couldn't you have shown a little discretion in front of him and his friends?"

Whenever Fay was frightened, she either exaggerated or got nasty. But this time she'd gone too far. Bristling with rage, Gideon rose to his feet.

"I'm on my way."

"That's good, because Kevin refuses to go home until you get here. He has this idea that you don't love him anymore, and he's afraid he'll never see you again.

"Frank can't do anything because Kevin doesn't respond to him. Our marriage has been fine until now. I tell you I can't handle this, Gideon! You caused the problem. Now you've got to fix it."

He had a temporary solution. In her highly vulnerable state, she might just agree. It was worth a shot.

"I know he's supposed to be with you today, but under the circumstances, how would you feel about letting him spend the day with me? It'll give us a chance to talk things over. We didn't have enough time last night."

"That's fine with me, as long as you make sure he doesn't have a reaction like this again."

"I can't promise that, Fay."

"Then Kevin was right."

"What do you mean?"

"He says you're going to marry her."

The way he felt about Heidi Ellis, it wasn't outside the realm of possibility.

"I don't know that yet."

"Well, well. This is quite a surprise."

Gideon supposed it was.

He let out the breath he'd been holding. Since their divorce, he'd known that Fay maintained the fiction that he'd never remarried because no woman had ever measured up to her. Kevin's revelation must have dealt her ego a significant blow.

She loved their son, but he realized she wasn't as shaken up by Kevin's present condition as by Gideon's finally finding a woman who, in Fay's mind, was her equal. She must've been consumed by curiosity.

Marriage meant Kevin would have a stepmother. No one was more competitive than Gideon's ex-wife. Her next comment confirmed his thoughts.

"When things get back to normal, you'll have to bring her to the house for cocktails."

"It's early days yet, Fay. Right now my concern is for Kevin. Tell him I'll be there as soon as I can."

A half hour later Gideon arrived at St. Anne's. Fay and her husband were standing outside the cubicle. The curtain had been pulled aside.

"Frank." Gideon nodded at him, then Fay, then hurried in to see his son, who was sitting on the edge of the exam table fully dressed.

"Hi, Dad," Kevin said in a tremulous voice. The glittering anger had gone from his eyes, thank God.

A lump swelled in Gideon's throat as he moved to embrace his little boy. Except that Kevin wasn't a little boy anymore. He was well on the way to manhood. That was the reality. It changed the way Gideon would have to deal with him from now on.

Kevin's arms went around him.

"I'm sorry, Dad. I didn't mean all those things," he said quietly, burying his face in Gideon's chest.

"And I'm sorry you felt so ill. How's your stomach now?"

"A little better."

"That's good. How would you like to spend the rest of the day with me?"

Kevin lifted his head. A glimmer of light had returned to his eyes. "Will Mom let me?"

"I already cleared it with her."

"Great," he said shyly. He slid off the table and ran out to give his mother a goodbye hug. Gideon followed at a brief distance.

"I'll have him home in plenty of time for bed," he told her. "Okay, Kevin. Let's go."

They left the emergency room and walked through the doors to the parking lot. Closer to the car they heard barking.

"Pokey!" Kevin's face broke into a smile, the first Gideon had seen since Friday. "You brought him!"

"He knew you needed cheering up."

Kevin climbed into the front seat and hugged his dog, who greeted him with unbridled enthusiasm.

Halfway to Ocean Beach his son appeared to be back to his normal self. Before they reached the house, there were things that needed to be discussed. Depending on the outcome of this conversation, Gideon would know what to say when he phoned Heidi.

"Kevin? I need to talk to you about something." His son flashed him a wary glance. "Do me a favor and listen without interrupting until I'm finished? Then you can ask all the questions you want."

"Okay."

"Thank you." Taking a deep breath, Gideon began. "Heidi Ellis's best friend, Dana Turner, is in prison for a murder Heidi claims she didn't commit."

Kevin's brown eyes widened in surprise. So far, so good.

"She and Dana grew up next door to each other. They're more like sisters than friends. Even though the case is closed, Heidi is so certain her friend is innocent, she's determined to find new evidence that will set her free.

"She signed up for Daniel's class in the hope of enlisting his help. Instead, she got me for a teacher.

"From the very first, we both felt an attraction. It wasn't something either of us planned. I have no idea if my feelings for her will grow or die. But so far, I like being around her very much.

"One day you'll grow up and fall in love. You'll get married and probably have kids. But your family— your mother and I—will still be part of your life.

"I'm at a stage where I'd like to find a woman who'll share my life, too. Maybe Heidi's that woman. Maybe she isn't. But my feelings for her are strong enough that I need to find out.

"Today I'd planned to drive her to the prison in San Bernardino so I could meet her friend. I'll be honest with you. I made those plans mostly because I wanted to be with Heidi. But I also wanted to talk to Dana. If my instincts tell me something's wrong, then I'm going to conduct my own investigation to see if some critical evidence was overlooked.

"Now, having said all that, would you like to drive to the prison with us? We'll bring Pokey. You can take him for a walk while I'm in the prison.

"If you don't want to come, I'll call Heidi and tell

her I'll go to the prison with her another time. What's important to me is that you and I be together today.

"Before you answer, keep in mind that if you come with us, you can get to know Heidi a little better. It's very important to me that you two get along. If you don't like her after you get to know her, then we'll talk about it."

He stared at his son. "That was a long speech, probably the longest you've ever had to sit through without saying anything. Now it's your turn."

A long silence. Finally Kevin said, "I'll go to the prison with you."

Gideon expelled the breath he'd been holding. Clearing his throat, he said, "You know what? I think you're a pretty terrific son."

Kevin eyed him steadily. "She probably hates me after the way I acted."

"Not at all."

"Frank doesn't like me."

"He thinks you're great. But he's scared of you."

"Scared?"

It was time Kevin understood the truth about a few things. "That's right. He's afraid that if he does anything to upset you, your mother won't love *him* anymore."

Kevin blinked. Obviously that was something he'd never considered. He remained silent until they reached the house.

As soon as Heidi saw the Acura from the window, she locked her apartment and ran out to the car, carrying her briefcase. While she'd been in the shower,

Gideon had left a brief voice message. As planned, he'd be by at ten. With Kevin.

She realized that whatever happened today would set the climate for the future. Knowing this, she was terrified of making a wrong move around Kevin.

If she tried to act like a pal, he'd ignore her. If she tried to mother him, he'd take offense. Acting like a schoolteacher would only annoy him. That didn't leave any options, because she'd be wrong no matter what she did. All she could do was follow his father's lead.

Gideon had to be twelve or thirteen years older than she was. The age difference didn't matter. But the fact that there was a fourteen-year history with his son *did.*

If Kevin never grew to like her, that animosity could taint a relationship with his father, even kill it. For personal reasons she had very real fears about the outcome of today's trip.

As for Dana, five minutes with her would convince Gideon that her friend wasn't capable of murder.

Gideon was just climbing out of the car when he saw her. Kevin immediately got out, too, holding a dog in his arms. No doubt his father had told him to sit in the back, the first of many things his son would naturally resent.

"Hi, you two."

"Good morning," came the deep, familiar voice. Gideon's eyes did a slow inventory of her face and figure—and she found herself doing the same to him. The dog barked, distracting her.

"So this is Pokey. Is he friendly?"

Kevin nodded.

She stroked the beagle's head and was rewarded with a lick on the hand. "He looks like Snoopy."

Her comment produced a faint smile.

She glanced in Gideon's direction. "Do you mind if I sit in the back seat? I need to spread my things out so I can record test scores in my roll book. Might as well get the drudge work done now."

Gideon sent her a private message that said he knew exactly what she was doing and he approved. He opened the back door and held her briefcase as she climbed inside.

She trembled from the brush of his hand against her thigh as he handed her the case. The effect was electrifying. He felt it, too. Their eyes met again, and the longing in his took her breath away.

He shut the door and moved around to the driver's seat. She decided to wait until they reached the freeway to take out her papers. For now she was content to gaze at the houses speeding by as they drove through the treed residential neighborhoods.

At one point she caught Gideon studying her in the rearview mirror. "You're awfully quiet back there."

She smiled at him. "I do too much talking in class. It's heavenly to just relax and be chauffeured around— even if it's by the police."

He laughed outright, and she felt ridiculously pleased.

"It's funny, isn't it?" she went on. "When you're Kevin's age, you think how exciting it's going to be when you can drive a car. Then after you get your license and you've been driving for a while, you realize what a luxury it is to let someone else do the work."

More laughter on Gideon's part. Heidi had no idea whether Kevin was paying any attention to her comments. More important was that he not feel she was ignoring him completely.

When they reached the freeway, she opened her briefcase and pulled out the tests she'd corrected. In another compartment she found her roll book and began the monotonous procedure of transferring grades.

Out of the corner of her eye, she saw a blond head turn her way. "How come you don't use a computer for your grades?"

Pleased that Kevin had been curious enough to ask, she paused in her work. "I do. But last year a student hacker broke into the teachers' computer files and changed a lot of the grades just before report cards were printed. It was a real nightmare, and I learned a good lesson about keeping my own hard copy up-to-date."

"Oh."

They drove another ten miles before he turned around again. This time Pokey's head popped up, too.

"What class are those for?"

"My ninth-graders. Geography."

"I'll be taking geography next year."

"What's your favorite class right now?"

"Earth science."

"With the right teacher that can be exciting."

"Mr. Harris is fun. He went to Mexico and brought us back chocolate-covered insects to eat."

"Mmm. Delicious. What did you choose?"

"A grasshopper."

"And you're still alive…. Congratulations."

Kevin forgot not to smile. It provoked the same response from his father, who glanced at her in the rearview mirror once again.

They made several gas-station stops en route. Kevin took Pokey for walks on his leash and let him drink from his water bowl. When they reached San Bernardino, Gideon decided they'd get hamburgers at a drive-through so the dog wouldn't have to be left alone in the car.

Everything remained pleasant and very low-key.

After lunch they left the city and headed into the San Bernardino mountains. A few miles out there was a turnoff for Fielding Women's Prison.

Heidi had been enjoying herself so much that seeing that sign was like being hit in the stomach with a baseball bat. She couldn't help feeling guilty that her life was this wonderful while Dana was locked in prison.

The outer perimeter of the building was surrounded by a concrete parking area, searchlights and an electric fence. There wasn't a tree in sight. Armed guards did sentry duty at the main gate. A huge sign had been posted:

Fielding Women's Prison Visiting Hours, Saturday and Sunday, 9 to 3.

Five visitors at a time. You must pass through the visitor processing center to be searched.

Requirements: No wigs, no sandals, no bandannas, no transparent blouses, no bra tops, no spaghetti straps, no blue, brown or forest-green clothes, no key chains, no Polaroids. Buy food and cigarettes inside. Forty dollars maximum is allowed in five-dollar increments.

Gideon showed his ID to the guard who'd asked him to state his business. Heidi had to give him her official permission slip. She was continually making applications to see Dana. They had to be submitted in writing five weeks ahead of each visit.

The electric gate opened to allow them through. There were dozens of cars parked near the processing center.

The Turners saw their daughter every Saturday. Though Sundays were the busiest days for visitors, Heidi always came then; she wanted to spread out the visits so Dana's week wouldn't seem so long. More often than not Heidi's parents accompanied her.

After Gideon pulled to a stop, Heidi started to leave the car when he said, "If you don't mind, I'd like to go in first."

Surprised—and a little chagrined because she'd wanted to tell Dana she'd brought an unexpected visitor—Heidi checked her movements and sat back again. "Of course. That's fine with me," she said quietly.

"Good." He smiled at Kevin. "I'll be back soon."

The shift in Gideon's mood was subtle, but it was there. The detective, not the man, was about to come face-to-face with a woman who'd been sent to prison for murder. Except for Heidi's assertions of her friend's innocence, he had no reason to believe there'd been a miscarriage of justice.

She watched him reach the building in a few swift

strides. When he disappeared inside, she closed her eyes tightly.

What if, after talking to her friend, he decided there was no case? What if this had all been for nothing? *Dear God.* Poor Dana…

Hot tears slipped beneath Heidi's lashes and trickled down her cheeks. A sob welled in her throat. Soon she was crying uncontrollably.

Until she heard the dog moan in humanlike fashion, she'd forgotten she wasn't alone.

"Ms. Ellis?"

"Uh-huh?"

Embarrassed to have lost control in front of Kevin, she wiped away her tears with both hands, then lifted her head.

"Do you want to take a walk with Pokey?" he asked solemnly.

She cleared her throat. "If we can all go together."

"Sure."

While he and the dog climbed out of the front seat, she got out of the back.

"Dad told me about your friend. Were you crying because of her?"

"I'm sorry, Kevin." She gulped in a breath. "I do this all the time over Dana's situation. Today I…suddenly felt this terror that your father won't feel there's anything he can do for her. It certainly won't be his fault.

"He was kind enough to come to the prison in the first place, but the chances of turning up something that will reopen her case are slim to none, as they say."

Kevin didn't respond. She didn't expect him to.

They started walking. Pokey took the lead, straining at his leash. Kevin went where he led; she followed.

GIDEON SAT IN FRONT of the glass while he waited for Dana to be brought in. He knew he'd taken Heidi by surprise in reversing the order of their visits. But since Dana didn't know about him, he wanted the chance to catch her off guard and had purposely asked the prison matron to withhold his name and title.

Since he had only the facts from Heidi's synopsis to go on, this first meeting was crucial. Over the years Gideon had discovered that a surprise visit to an unsuspecting inmate or witness often allowed him a glimpse into the other person's psyche.

Many crimes were solved on a hunch, a premonition, an instinct. Gideon didn't plan to overlook anything. Clearly any hope for a future with Heidi was jeopardized as long as Dana's life hung in the balance.

In his desire for an advantage in this meeting, he hadn't counted on being thrown a curve, but that was what it felt like when a tall, beautiful brunette came slowly toward him. Though she was underweight, she made the denim-blue prison shift look like a fashion statement.

It wasn't until she sat down that he noticed the gauntness of her face. Her gray eyes lacked luster. There were shadows and lines that shouldn't have been there, not on a woman who was only in her mid-twenties.

Heidi was right; her friend's fragility was shocking. Prison life had definitely taken its toll. Gideon had the grim conviction that Dana Turner would not survive long behind bars.

He picked up the phone receiver and waited for her to do the same. As soon as she sat down, he said, "Hello, Dana."

"Hello," she said in a tremulous voice. She sounded like a frightened child rather than a woman capable of murdering her sister in cold blood. "Are you one of the attorneys from Mr. Cobb's office?"

"No. My name is Gideon Poletti. I'm a criminal investigator with the San Diego Police Department."

She stared at him as if he were an apparition.

"Through an unusual set of circumstances," he went on, "I was asked to teach a night class in criminology for the adult-education department. It's being held in Heidi Ellis's room at Mesa Junior High. She joined the class. That's how I learned about you."

Suddenly tears spurted from her eyes. In the next breath she covered her face with her free hand and started to sob. Those sobs came straight from her soul and they tugged at his emotions.

"I-I'm sorry," she said a few moments later when she'd regained control of herself. "It's just that Heidi said she'd have something good to report the next time she came. She's been my guardian angel, but I never expected her to hire a det—"

She broke off. A look of pain crossed her face. "If I've misunderstood, please forgive me."

"Heidi didn't have to hire me," he assured her. "She told me about your case and says you're innocent. I came today because I'd like to ask you some questions."

"Of course." She wiped her eyes. "Anything."

"I don't have a lot of time this morning, so why don't you just tell me about the relationship with your sister? Why did the two of you get into a physical fight the night she was killed?"

She hunched her shoulders. "Until Amy started junior high, she was the sweetest girl, studious and a little on the quiet side. We were good friends and got along well.

"Then it seemed as though she went through this personality change overnight. She became moody and explosive. Instead of talking to me like she always had, she would either ignore me or pick a fight. There was no in-between.

"Mom and Dad were alarmed because she'd turned into a secretive person who stopped doing things with the family and never brought her friends home.

"My parents took her for counseling, but after several sessions she refused to go anymore. Her schoolwork suffered. The only class she liked in high school was drama. She said she wanted to be a movie star.

"By that time my parents were desperate to help her in any way they could. They decided to enroll her in a special acting school in San Diego. She'd be able to pick up credits to graduate from high school, but the main emphasis would be on acting.

"She still lived at home, but the environment threw her in with a crowd of teens Mom and Dad didn't get the opportunity to even meet. She started to dress differently, do strange things with her hair and makeup. Amy became a law unto herself. We're pretty sure she began hanging around with some questionable people.

"After graduation she drove to Los Angeles with a few other girls, in the hope of getting into a renowned acting school where various Hollywood film stars got their start. Though Mom and Dad worried about that decision, they were willing to pay her expenses if she got in.

"But there was one problem. She had to pass a difficult audition first. Unfortunately neither she nor her two friends from acting school made the grade. The three of them were urged to take more dance and speech classes, then try out again the next year.

"I knew she was crushed about being turned down, but to my surprise, she and her friends joined another acting school here in San Diego. Mom and Dad were relieved because it meant she'd still be at home where they'd have at least some contact with her.

"On the night she was killed, I was in my parents' study writing a term paper on the computer."

"What time was that?"

"Around eight o'clock. When she walked in, I was surprised because I thought I was alone in the house. Before I could even say hi, she accused me of trashing her room.

"I couldn't imagine what she was talking about. She told me to come to her bedroom and see, so I did. When I got there, I was shocked. The room looked as if a tornado had swept through it.

"My first thought was that someone had entered the house and could still be inside. I told her we needed to call the police. But when I reached for the phone, she flew at me and knocked the receiver out of my hand.

"She'd never done anything like this before. That's when I knew something was really wrong with her. She stood there like a demented person and raged at me, accusing me of stealing her diaries.

"I had no idea what she was talking about, since I didn't even know she kept a diary. But she was beyond listening to me. She lunged for me again. I couldn't believe how strong she was!"

"Stronger than normal?"

"I don't know because we'd never fought before."

"You mean physically."

"Yes. She grabbed my hair and yanked it hard. I lost my balance and fell on the floor. If you could've seen her eyes... She *enjoyed* hitting me. The more I tried to protect myself, the harder she fought.

"I was terrified she wouldn't quit until I was unconscious. Finally I managed to roll far enough to the side to kick her off balance. Then I got up and started running.

"The back door was closest, so I dashed out it and ran to the pier. I got into our boat, knowing I'd be safe on the water. But it must've been out of gas because the motor wouldn't turn over."

"So you pushed off before she caught up to you?"

"Ye— No." She changed words so fast that if he hadn't been listening for the smallest slip, he wouldn't have caught it. "I had no idea how close she was to me. All I knew was that I wanted to get as far away from the house as possible.

"I jumped off the boat and ran along the beach until I was exhausted. After sitting on the sand for a couple of hours, I circled back to the house to see if Mom and Dad had come home yet.

"To my horror, I saw police cars and fire engines out in front. All the neighbors had crowded around. The air smelled of smoke. You know the rest. The police accused me of knocking her unconscious, then setting her room on fire." Her voice fell to a mere whisper.

"Is that what the autopsy report said? She was overcome by smoke inhalation?"

Her face glistened with tears. "There was no autopsy."

"*What?*" Gideon blinked. "Why? Was it against your family's religion?"

"No. The evidence against me was apparently conclusive. It was determined that no autopsy was required, especially since my parents couldn't stand the thought of...of Amy's body being cut open. Neither could I."

Good Lord. If Gideon had been the detective on this case, he would've insisted on an autopsy paid for by the department.

"I'm sorry to make you relive that night, Dana, but it's essential if I'm going to investigate your case."

He heard her sharp gasp. "Then you believe I didn't kill my sister?"

Gideon felt in his gut that she was innocent, but he needed to be cruel if he was going to get anywhere on this case.

"Yes, but I also believe that part of your story is a lie."

"What do you mean?" she cried.

"Exactly what I said." He stood up. "When you're ready to talk, let me know through Heidi."

"Wait! Please—don't go!"

"If you can't be totally honest with me, there's nothing more to discuss. You're already serving your sentence, so I know you're not lying to save your own skin. Which means you're lying to save someone else's. Until you come clean, further conversation would be a waste of your time and mine."

By now she was on her feet. He didn't know how it was possible, but her face had gone even whiter.

"You won't come again?"

"Not unless you give me a good reason."

He could feel how torn she was between wanting to remain silent and her need to disclose what she'd been hiding.

"It was nice meeting you, Dana."

He started to hang up the receiver but she called him back.

"Please don't leave yet. I-I'll tell you, but you have to promise this conversation won't go any further than the two of us."

Elation swept through him. Now he was getting somewhere. "I can't make you a promise like that, not if I'm going to help you."

The pain in her eyes couldn't possibly have been fabricated. "Then there's nothing more for me to say except thank you for coming. Please tell Heidi I appreciate her effort, but the truth is, I don't want her worrying about me anymore. It would be better if she didn't come to see me again."

Before he could respond, she'd hung up and disappeared.

He remained there in a quandary.

No autopsy, and Dana Turner was protecting someone.

What person was so important to her that she preferred to stay behind bars and refuse Gideon's help in order to retain her secret?

Aware that there were other visitors impatient for their turn to talk to an inmate, he headed out of the building. On the way to the car he felt that familiar rush of adrenaline.

Like a hunter who'd suddenly picked up the scent, Gideon wouldn't be able to let this go now—even if he didn't have a personal stake in the outcome.

CHAPTER SEVEN

IT WASN'T DIFFICULT for Heidi to spot Gideon in a crowd. With his height, dark hair and rugged features, he always stood out. He was especially noticeable in the red-plaid flannel shirt and black trousers he was wearing today.

Kevin and Pokey must have seen him at the same moment. The dog barked with excitement as they hurried across the parking lot toward him. Heidi followed at a short distance, giving Kevin time to greet his father first.

When she walked up to the car, Gideon was patting the dog while Kevin rummaged in the glove compartment and retrieved a couple of wrapped mints. Her mouth had gone dry from fear that Gideon would tell her he wasn't convinced of Dana's innocence.

He lifted his head to look at her. She couldn't read anything in his expression. "Sorry I was gone so long."

"We didn't notice the time," she murmured. "Pokey does wonderful tricks. Kevin put him through every conceivable maneuver for me. The best one was when the dog raised his paw to shake my hand."

"Pokey won't do that for people who aren't dog lovers," Gideon informed her.

"How could anyone not love this little guy?" She stooped to scratch behind his ears. The dog inched closer to rub against her legs.

"I think we've been here long enough. What do you say we all go home?"

Gideon's unexpected suggestion brought a sharp pain to her chest. Before she could form words, he said, "We took a little longer to get here. Unfortunately visiting hours are almost over and the late-Sunday-afternoon traffic is going to be heavy. I think we'd better leave now if we want to get back at a decent hour. Shall we go?"

"Yes, of course," Heidi agreed, but her heart wasn't in it. Avoiding Gideon's eyes, she turned and opened the rear door of the car before he could suggest she ride in the front. For her own sake, she needed to put distance between herself and Gideon.

He was probably trying to decide how best to put the bad news to her and didn't want Kevin to be a witness. For that matter, he must know it would be devastating to Dana if Heidi went inside the visitors' center and fell apart. Just as well that visiting hours were almost over.

Kevin offered her a mint, which Heidi declined. Then he got in the front seat with Pokey. There was an uneasy silence as his father climbed behind the wheel and started the engine.

After the guard checked them at the gate, Gideon switched on the radio, turning it to an easy-listening station, and they were off. It was another not-so-subtle trick of his to prevent unwanted conversation.

The dog kept looking over the seat, whining softly. Kevin turned around. "Do you want him in the back?"

Despite his hostility toward her at the restaurant yesterday, Heidi had been prepared to like Kevin. She was relieved that today he'd been civil with her, even pleasant.

"I was hoping you'd offer. Come here, Pokey," she urged. "Come on, boy." Kevin helped his dog over the seat. Pokey moved around for a minute, then lay down, dropping his head in her lap. She began to rub behind his ears. There was comfort in the dog's presence, in his solid warmth against her. She knew how consoling an animal could be for a confused, vulnerable teen like Kevin. Right now she was grateful for a little of that consolation herself.

"He thinks he's died and gone to dog heaven."

Though she avoided looking at Gideon in the rearview mirror, his comment brought a smile to her lips.

What is it you're keeping from me, Gideon? I thought you could make the miracle happen for Dana. I can't believe there isn't something *you can do.*

They made one rest stop to buy sandwiches and drinks. When they were ready to get back in the car, she arranged for the dog to sit in front with Kevin again.

During the rest of the drive she organized all the students' papers, then put everything away in her briefcase. As soon as she saw the sign for Mission Beach, she leaned forward.

"Will you drop me off first? I have more work to do on my computer tonight—stuff I need to finish before school in the morning."

Gideon flicked her an enigmatic glance. "I was going to suggest it."

She sat back, desperately trying not to show her hurt. When he stopped at the curb in front of her apartment, she sprang from the car.

Before shutting the door, she said, "You don't need to see me inside."

"I'll call you," was all Gideon said.

"Thanks for lunch and the trip. I enjoyed it. See you later, Pokey. Take care, Kevin."

"Bye."

She could hear the dog barking as she hurried along the path with her purse and briefcase. Unable to get into her apartment fast enough, she dashed up the stairs, key in hand. The Acura didn't drive away until she'd let herself in.

Beyond tears, she took off her suit and changed into jeans and a T-shirt. Slipping into loafers, she left the apartment for her parents' home in Mission Bay.

After meeting Gideon, she'd made the mistake of pinning all her hopes on him. Her parents needed to be informed that, wonderful though she thought he was, he probably wouldn't be able to help Dana, after all.

KEVIN SEEMED DISINCLINED to talk. Gideon feared his son was going to be difficult about returning to Fay's. The thought of a repeat of this morning's performance at the hospital left a coil of tension in his stomach.

"Dad? Can I ask you a question?"

"Of course."

"Why'd you make us come home before Ms. Ellis could go in to visit her friend?"

"Because I don't want the two of them talking yet."

"You think her friend killed her sister?"

"My instincts tell me no."

"Then who did?"

His son had grown up overnight. Gideon reminded himself again that he needed to treat Kevin in a more adult way.

"I have no idea. But I did learn one thing. Dana's withholding information no one knows about. Not even Heidi."

"How did you find that out?"

"Because I caught her in a lie. She said she'd level with me as long as I kept it a secret. But I couldn't promise that, so she closed up on me."

"How come she's afraid? She's already in prison."

"Exactly. It means she's protecting someone."

"Who?"

"I don't know, but I'm going to find out. Unfortunately, because of my probing, Dana got defensive on me. In fact, she said she didn't want Heidi to visit her anymore."

"That's why we left so fast?"

"Yes. I didn't want Heidi to go into the visitors' facility only to be told by the matron that Dana wouldn't talk to her."

His son's face went very still. "You really like her, don't you?"

"Yes," Gideon said honestly.

He hadn't known what to expect when he'd left the two of them alone. But it didn't sound as if Kevin had softened.

"What will you do now?"

"Before Heidi attempts to see Dana again, I need to find out how much she knows about the murder. Then I'll go downtown and read Dana's case from start to finish. After that I'll start my investigation."

"So you're going to work on it for her?" Kevin demanded.

Already damned for being interested in Heidi on a personal level, Gideon realized that in his son's eyes, agreeing to help her was making matters even worse. Aside from the issue of Kevin's jealousy, it meant more time spent away from him.

"Yes."

"Is she going to pay you?"

Good Lord. "I wouldn't take her money, Kevin."

His son squinted at him. It made him look older than his fourteen years. "Maybe Ms. Ellis had something to do with the murder and she's the one her friend's protecting."

This remark, intended to wound Gideon, lifted the hair on the back of his neck—particularly as the same thought had crossed his mind when he'd first gone to Daniel about the Turner case. Alarmed and saddened by Kevin's attitude, he had no words to calm a volatile situation.

They pulled up in front of the house without speaking. It didn't surprise Gideon that Fay immediately came outside. She was the main reason he hadn't wanted Heidi in the car. If his ex-wife had caught one glance of so much glorious red hair, she would've marched right down the path to talk to them, creating a confrontation Heidi wasn't ready for.

As it was, Fay had allowed one day's irregularity in

visitation, but that was it. She wanted their son in the house. Now.

Kevin had seen her, too. He opened the car door. Before getting out, he stroked the dog's head. "Be good, Pokey." He refused to look at Gideon.

"I'll see you on Wednesday right after school."

"That's okay, Dad. You've got other things to do." The door slammed shut.

Gideon groaned. Obviously nothing was going to be settled tonight—or anytime soon.

He watched until Kevin had gone in the house with Fay, then he took out his cell phone to call Heidi and tell her he was coming over. To his chagrin he got her voice mail.

"Heidi? It's Gideon. If you're there, please call me back on my cell." He gave her the number. "I took Kevin home and I'm on my way to your apartment. We have to talk."

He clicked off, then headed for her place. By the time he'd turned down her street, she still hadn't returned his call. The same light was on in her living room. Wondering if she was even there, he drove around to the back of her apartment building to the carports. Her Audi was missing.

Frustrated, he called again. "Heidi? I came by, but you weren't home. I need to take Pokey to my house, then I'm coming back. If you're not here, I'll wait for you."

He didn't know if she had a cell phone or not. Before the night was over he intended to find out. It was vital to his peace of mind that he be able to reach her no matter where she was.

"Come on, Pokey. Let's get you home. You've been cooped up long enough."

HEIDI'S PARENTS wouldn't let her wallow in disappointment because Gideon hadn't been able to tell her he would take Dana's case. Her father assured her there were other detectives they could hire. He would make inquiries at work the next day.

As he was vice president of AmerOil for Southern California, he would call in their company attorneys, who handled litigation problems, and get their suggestions. He felt sure someone would know a criminal investigator and make a referral they could follow up on.

She thanked him with a hug, then left for her apartment. But despite her father's promise, she had no peace.

Gideon wasn't the kind of man to lead her on when he knew he couldn't help Dana. She might not know him well, but she recognized that fundamental integrity in him. Furthermore, the last thing he'd want to do was discuss Dana in front of Kevin. The fact that he'd brought his son on the drive meant Kevin's state of mind was fragile.

Emotionally exhausted from trying to figure out the whole confusing mess, she decided it would be best to drop the night class. As long as her father was going to find another detective, there was no longer any point in attending.

To continue seeing Gideon would only increase her attraction to him and cause Kevin grief. The man might be unforgettable, but there were far too many complications. Some relationships just weren't meant to be.

After pulling into her carport, she hurried up the back stairs and let herself into the kitchen. Before she got ready for bed, she checked her messages.

Michael Ray had phoned to ask her out and wanted her to call him back at the first opportunity. He was a graduate student who'd been hired three weeks ago to work part-time at the furniture warehouse run by her mother's family. Heidi's first impression had been that he was a nice guy and not bad-looking. But she wasn't interested.

Since meeting Gideon Poletti, she couldn't entertain the thought of any other man in her life. Maybe she never would again. All she knew was that it would take a long time to work him out of her system.

As if thinking about him had conjured him up, the next voice message was from him. And the one after that.

Good heavens—he was outside? *Now?*

Heart pounding wildly, she swung around and ran through her apartment. Turning on the front porch light, she opened the door and saw him coming up the walk.

"Gideon!" She gasped. "I just heard your messages. I can't believe I didn't notice your car when I drove in."

He took the stairs two at a time. "You must've had other things on your mind."

You. You were on my mind. Everything else was a blur.

"May I come in?"

"Of course."

He moved inside and shut the door. "Why don't we go into your kitchen?"

"A-All right." Her stomach was in knots. She led him through the living room to the kitchen, urging him to take a place at the table. "How long have you been waiting out there?"

"Not long."

"I'm sorry." She rubbed the palms of her hands on her hips. "How was Kevin when you took him home?"

He eyed her intently. "He's not planning to come to class on Wednesday night."

It was worse than she'd thought. "I'm so sorry." She inhaled deeply, trying to quell her anxiety. "Can I get you something to eat or drink?"

"Not right now, thanks." His unrelenting gaze forced her to look at him. "Where did you go when I dropped you off?"

"My parents'."

He nodded. "Heidi…after talking to Dana, I'm convinced she didn't kill her sister."

Her world stood still for a moment. "You're not just telling me that because you know it's what I want to hear?"

"Not at all. I came to that conclusion while she was giving me her version of events. However, certain things didn't add up," he said cryptically. "At this point it's no longer a question of what anyone else wants. I believe the wrong person is behind bars. Therefore, I'm going to begin my own investigation."

"Oh, thank God!" she cried, clasping her hands.

Overjoyed by his words, she reached for her purse on the counter to get her checkbook. "I'll pay you a retainer and—"

"Put everything away, Heidi. I'm not interested in receiving a fee and couldn't accept one, anyway."

"But—"

"Listen," he said, cutting her off. "I thought I'd made it clear that I'm doing this to satisfy my own sense of justice as much as anything."

Her hand stilled on the purse.

"I know it's getting late and we both have work in the morning, but before I leave, I'd like to ask you a few questions about Dana's case."

There was a ring of steel in his voice that was slightly intimidating. "Of course."

"Why don't you sit down."

"All right." She sank onto the opposite chair.

"The other day you mentioned that Dana had an apartment."

She blinked. "Yes. Before she went to prison, she had a beautiful place. After she was sentenced, her parents stored her things and gave up the apartment."

"Where was it located?"

"Pasadena."

"Why there?"

"Dana was in graduate school at Caltech."

"What department?"

"She didn't tell you?"

"There wasn't time to get into a lot of background questions. What I wanted from her was an account of what she did the night of the murder. Now that I have her testimony, I'd like some answers from you."

Heidi let out a sigh. "I'm sorry. I don't mean to be difficult." She pushed a stray curl off her forehead. "Dana was studying physics and astronomy."

"That's impressive."

"She's the only reason I passed the one physics class I had to take at UCSD to get my teaching degree. She inherited her father's brain."

"Tell me about him."

"Dr. Turner's been one of the head astronomers at the Mount Palomar Observatory for quite a few years now."

He nodded. "Do you have any idea why Dana was at her parents' home the night of Amy's murder?"

Again Heidi started to ask him the reason for these questions when he'd already heard all this from Dana, but she caught herself.

"My school had just let out, so my parents asked me to keep an eye on their house while they went to New York for a week of furniture-buying. Dana had just finished her exams at Caltech, but she still had a paper to work on.

"I was anxious to see her, so I urged her to drive down and do it at her parents' house. We had a lot of catching up to do because she'd just been through a stormy relationship that didn't work out and she wanted to talk about it.

"Also, we were planning a trip to Mexico as soon as my parents got back. There were decisions we needed to make before finalizing our itinerary."

"Did you see Dana on the day Amy was killed?"

"You *know* I did!" she blurted. "You've already

discussed it with Dana.'' Her eyes slid away. ''Forgive me. That's the second time I've been rude to you.''

''It's all right,'' he said in a quiet voice. ''Just bear with me a little longer.''

She nodded. ''I'm sure Dana told you we both wanted to get started on a tan before leaving for Mexico, so we took my dad's rowboat out on the bay to picnic and sunbathe. We didn't go back to the pier until much later in the day.''

''Is that your parents' pier?''

''It's a pier shared by the Turners and my parents. They have an inboard ski boat.''

''I see. What did you do then?''

''Dana went inside to work on her paper. I had to go back to my apartment to get ready for a blind date. It'd been arranged by a teacher friend who'd been trying to talk me into it for the better part of a year. But at the last minute I couldn't go through with it and called the guy to break it. I figured he probably didn't want to go, either.''

''Instead, you found out that wasn't how he felt at all. He'd been looking forward to it, correct?''

She lifted her head to discover him studying her features. Her face went hot. ''Yes.''

''What happened then?''

''I should've just gone on that date with my friend's brother. By backing out of it, I turned everything into a huge mess. She called me up and told me exactly what she thought of me.

''I felt awful because she was right. It was a cruel thing to do.'' Heidi shrugged weakly. ''I had no excuse except that I guess a blind date just isn't for me. Anyway, I couldn't stand my own company, so I drove over to Dana's to see if she'd go out for a drive with me, even though I knew she was working on her paper."

"What time was that?"

"Around six-thirty. But when I got there and saw how much she still had to do, I realized I was just being selfish. So I went alone and told her I'd call her in the morning."

Barely holding on to her self-control, she added, "If only Dana had come with me that night, she wouldn't be in prison now."

"Not necessarily."

His comment made her shiver.

"Tell me about your drive. Where did you go?"

"I headed for the hills like I usually do."

"Where, precisely?"

"There's a monastery near the Mount Palomar Observatory. Over the years I've often driven up that way because it's so quiet and beautiful."

"Did you go alone?"

"Yes."

"Did you stop anywhere?"

"No."

"No one saw you?"

She frowned. "Not that I know of. By the time I got that far, I was tired, so I turned around and drove back to my apartment. Gideon...why does it matter where I went?"

"I'm attempting to get a sense of the circumstances that night. When did you find out what had happened at the Turner house?"

"The next morning I phoned Dana so we could go down to the travel agency. I was planning to drive over to my parents' house, take the mail and newspaper inside, then pick her up."

"Where were you?"

"You mean when I phoned?"

"Yes."

"At my apartment."

"Go on."

"Dr. Turner answered and told me the awful news." Hot tears sprang to her eyes. "When I heard that Dana had been arrested for Amy's murder, my world fell apart. I didn't see her until she'd been released on bail. None of our lives have been the same since."

"It must've been very difficult for you on the witness stand."

She stared hard at him, not understanding. "I didn't attend her trial."

He rubbed his thumb across his bottom lip. "While I was at the prison, Dana and I didn't have time to discuss what happened in court. I didn't realize you weren't called to testify."

"I begged her to let me and my family be character witnesses for her, but she wouldn't allow it. Dana said she didn't want to drag us into her problems."

"John Cobb should've insisted that you take the stand."

Heidi tried in vain to swallow the lump in her throat. "I felt so helpless. That's why I came to your class. I couldn't stand by any longer and do nothing!

"Please let me pay you for investigating her case. I

won't feel right about it otherwise. Neither will my parents.''

He shook his head. ''Whatever I do for Dana will be on my own time. And as I told you, my most compelling reason for taking it on is a desire to see justice done.''

Pushing himself away from the table, he got to his feet. ''When I've found evidence that could result in this case being reopened, I'll meet with Dana's attorney. Until then, everything is still unofficial.''

Before she could take another breath, he'd walked into the living room. She caught up with him at the front door. ''Gideon, I don't expect you to spend your precious time off working for free!''

His mouth curved into a slow smile. ''I said I wouldn't take money, but that doesn't mean I won't expect payment.''

If he was saying what she suspected he was saying…

''Your thoughts are transparent, Ms. Ellis.''

Heat scorched her cheeks.

''I'm talking about time,'' he said. ''*Your* time, spent with me.'' He reached out to caress her throat with one finger. ''I'm making you my assistant. That means we get together as often as possible to gather evidence and collaborate. I'll pick you up for dinner at five-thirty tomorrow evening. Shall we try that Mexican place again?''

Heidi was trembling so hard she couldn't speak.

''I'll take that as a yes.''

The brush of his lips against hers burned like fire long after he'd left.

CHAPTER EIGHT

GIDEON RODE the elevator to the subbasement of headquarters. When he entered the reception area, Ben, a retired street cop, waved him over to the counter.

"It's been a while, Gideon."

"Yeah, Ben. How are you?"

"Couldn't be better."

I feel the same way.

Gideon had barely touched Heidi at the door last night, but it was enough for him to know the strong chemistry between them hadn't been a figment of his imagination. He'd be seeing her tonight, but at seven in the morning, that still seemed a long time off.

"The boss told me you were on your way down. What case do you need?"

"The Amy Turner murder brief."

"Do you remember the trial date?"

"Sometime last August. Ron Jenke prosecuted it. The attorney for the defendant was John Cobb."

Ben looked it up on the computer, then glanced at Gideon. "What all do you want?"

"Read me the list."

"Besides the official records and court transcript, there's a set of six diaries and an envelope containing items from the deceased's handbag."

"Let me see everything."

"Okay. Back in a minute.

While Gideon waited, he made a call to the county coroner's office to finalize plans for Wednesday night's class. Given that it was a couple of days away, he could only hope that Kevin would change his mind and agree to come.

Being on the outs with his son was a painful experience. One sure way to remedy the situation was to stop seeing Heidi altogether, but for too many reasons, personal and otherwise, Gideon wasn't prepared to do that. Already he recognized that she was someone of vital importance in his life.

In any event, ending things with her wouldn't solve Kevin's deeper problem. The truth was that any woman Gideon cared about would threaten his son's emotional security. Only time would reveal if Kevin needed more therapy.

Fay hated it that a few years ago Gideon had insisted on getting their son professional help to deal with his fears. She claimed not to believe in psychotherapy—no doubt because some of her own actions didn't bear much scrutiny.

Gideon suspected that she was petrified of a psychologist working with Kevin at this point. It might change the fragile balance between mother and son. Now that Kevin was a teenager making noises about wanting to live with his father, Fay was terrified of where therapy might lead. Gideon knew she wanted to maintain the status quo at all costs; losing control of her son would undermine her carefully constructed sense of self.

"Here you are."

Brought back to the present, Gideon turned toward the older man.

"Just sign this slip, then you can use room A."

"Thanks." After putting his signature on the line, Gideon gathered the material and carried it to the first empty cubicle beyond the door Ben had unlocked for him.

He set everything on the table. The heavy folder contained the legal documents, which had been separated into alphabetized sections.

Gideon had only intended to scan the materials before he went on duty in an hour, but by the time he'd finished reading the incident report, he was too engrossed to stop.

Pulling out his cell phone, he called Rich Taggert, the detective working with him on the murder case assigned to them last week. He explained that he'd gotten tied up with unfinished business and would be late meeting him at their rendezvous point.

Rich was fine about it. They agreed to catch up with each other later in the morning. Relieved to be given a few more hours, Gideon thanked his partner, then got to work.

When he'd gone through the envelope, he became immersed in the various documents and lost track of time.

"Good Lord," he muttered at the end of the court transcript. If ever a case looked airtight, this was it.

Stunned by what he'd read, he reached for the cream-colored diaries with gold scrollwork borders and began reading in chronological order.

When he'd finished the last volume, he shoved away from the table and picked everything up. Arms full, he hurried into the reception area.

"Thanks for the materials, Ben."

The older man checked them off. "You bet."

Too impatient to wait for the elevator outside the doors, Gideon ran up the stairs to Lieutenant Rodman's office on the third floor. He still found it hard to walk in there and not find Daniel sitting at the desk.

The lieutenant raised his head when he saw Gideon enter the room. "Did you get what you needed from Ben?"

"I did. Thanks."

"Daniel said it was important."

"It is." Gideon paused for a moment. "Do you have a minute to talk?"

"Of course. Take a seat."

Gideon hooked his leg over a chair and sat down. "I'll get straight to the point."

"You always do," the other man said with a smile. "What's on your mind?"

"I'd like to be taken off the Simonds murder case."

Lieutenant Rodman cocked his head. "You and Rich don't get along?"

"That's not the problem. I have a lot of respect for Rich. There's no better man." Gideon sat forward. "Lieutenant, I'm going to be frank with you. By sheer accident, I've become involved with a woman who's convinced that her best friend has been wrongfully imprisoned for murder."

"You're referring to the Turner case."

Gideon nodded. "I'd like permission to investigate it."

"A closed case?"

"Yes."

The other man released a low whistle. Gideon had been expecting that reaction.

"On what evidence?"

"Yesterday I went to the prison to talk to Dana Turner. During our conversation, I caught her out in a lie. She refused to say any more and immediately left the visiting area.

"I figured she was protecting someone. After poring over her court records this morning, I came across the proof I was looking for. Dana Turner lied under oath to protect someone else."

The lieutenant's eyes narrowed. "Are you saying there could be an accessory here?"

"That's what it looks like on the surface. But my gut instinct tells me there's a different explanation. Ron Jenke was in such a hurry to nail another prosecution before the election, he didn't do all his homework. I'd like to pick up where he left off."

Lieutenant Rodman sat back in the swivel chair. "How much time are we talking about?"

"How much time can you give me?"

"Not much. Right now we've got a dozen cases, including the Simonds murder, that need your expertise."

Gideon felt his shrewd regard.

"This woman you met must mean a hell of a lot to you."

Heidi's image flashed before his eyes. "It's taken me by surprise, believe me."

Silence stretched between them.

"All right. You've got one week to see where this goes. I have to be able to justify your using the department's time to dig up old ground. If you haven't come up with compelling evidence by then, you'll have to do any further investigation on your off hours."

One week.

"Thanks, Lieutenant," he said with heartfelt gratitude. "I'm indebted to you."

"Tell the sergeant you and I talked. He can hook Rich up with someone else. Oh, and Gideon? Let's keep this between ourselves. For what it's worth, I hope you get lucky."

Amen to that. "May I ask a couple more favors?"

"Go ahead."

"I need photocopies of the court transcript and diaries in Amy Turner's file. I'll swing by here to pick them up after I get back from the prison."

"You've got it. What else?"

"Would you mind phoning the warden at Fielding Prison to get me immediate clearance? It's nine-thirty. If I leave now, I can be there before lunch."

A request from the lieutenant would cut through all the red tape. Dana would have no choice but to talk to Gideon.

"I'll do it right now."

"Thanks again." They shook hands.

After checking in with the sergeant, Gideon left headquarters feeling a sense of purpose and excitement he hadn't experienced in years. While he stopped for gas, he phoned Rich and told him the lieutenant had given him a week's personal leave for something he had to take care of.

Rich wasn't the type to pry. They talked business for a few minutes, then ended the call.

Two hours later Gideon found himself in front of the glass partition at the prison, waiting for Dana to appear. It was exactly like the previous day—with one difference. This morning he was armed with crucial information he hadn't known yesterday. With that kind of leverage, Dana Turner wouldn't be running away from him again.

At his first sight of her, he noticed that the bruised look beneath her eyes was more pronounced than it had been the day before. He could tell she hadn't slept. Her movements were wooden as she sat down. The prison matron was forced to pick up the receiver and put it in Dana's hand.

"Dana?" Gideon spoke into his receiver. She still refused to look at him. "You don't have to say anything yet. Just listen to me.

"Last night I had a long talk with Heidi. Among other things, I found out she didn't testify at your trial. According to Heidi, you told her and her parents to stay away and wouldn't let your attorney call them as character witnesses.

"That sent up a red flag, but I didn't say anything to Heidi. In fact, she has no idea I'm here."

He saw Dana's hands clench and unclench.

"First thing this morning," he continued, "I went to headquarters to look over your case in the archives.

I've read the court transcript and your sister's diaries. It's clear as day that you've been protecting Heidi.

"After what she told me last night, plus what I read earlier today, I believe there's enough circumstantial evidence for Ron Jenke to bring her in for questioning right now."

Dana's head reared back. He was startled by the terrified expression in her eyes.

"I know she was at your parents' house on the night the murder took place. She didn't mention seeing Amy, and no one else is aware she was even there.

"She can't prove she didn't have a physical fight with your sister. To make matters worse, she says she went for a drive during the time the murder took place. But she can't prove that, either."

He pinned Dana with his gaze. "You knew she didn't have an alibi for that night, so you made sure you never brought up her name. From the very beginning you lied in every conceivable way to protect her."

"Yes!" Dana cried at last.

Now he was getting somewhere. He indicated to the matron standing nearby that they needed privacy.

When the matron obliged by moving away, he asked, "How is it the police didn't include Heidi and her family when they interviewed the neighbors?"

"I told them the Ellises were in New York on a business trip and that Heidi had moved to an apartment at least five years earlier. I also said I hadn't seen anyone in their family for a couple of months because I'd been away at school in Pasadena."

"Thank you for being honest with me. Now let's finish what we started yesterday. Why don't you begin with the point at which you ran to your boat and realized it was out of gas.''

Dana looked ill.

''Let me help you. When I asked if you'd pushed off before Amy caught up to you, you started to say yes, then you changed your story. According to the court transcript, you testified that you ran along the beach.''

She nodded.

''What really happened? Just tell me the truth.''

He watched her shift restlessly. ''I got away in the Ellises' rowboat. I was so terrified of Amy, who was a strong swimmer, that I rowed to the other end of the bay and stayed there for several hours.

''When I thought Mom and Dad would have returned, I left the boat on a stretch of beach, then walked home. You know e-everything else,'' she stammered.

Surely someone had discovered the rowboat. He'd discuss that with Heidi later.

''Now that you've been honest with me, I'll return the courtesy. Since I'm a homicide detective, I have to admit I was more than a little curious when Heidi used a real murder case for her writing assignment.

''Even though it was fleeting, the notion that she might be involved in Amy's murder did enter my mind. It's only natural. After all, I've been trained to assume that anything's possible.

''But as time went on, it became clear to me Heidi had joined the class in order to get help for you.'' He shook his head. ''I'd never met a person who showed as much love for a friend as Heidi did for you. Now here I am, looking at the woman who committed per-

jury to protect Heidi, to keep her out of this mess....
You're both quite remarkable.''

Tears filled her eyes. ''I can't explain why we're so
close. We just are.''

''At what point did you decide Heidi could be im-
plicated?''

''Before I got back to the house that night, Mom and
Dad overheard the investigating officer tell another officer that he thought Amy had been murdered. Everyone in our house was under suspicion.

''Dad realized what that meant, so he called a friend
who got hold of Mr. Cobb. He agreed to be our family's attorney and advised all of us to keep quiet until
he could talk to us.

''The minute my dad saw me, he warned me not to
answer any questions until Mr. Cobb was present. I was
terrified for Heidi because I knew she'd been at our
house earlier. Luckily no one knew about that, so I
purposely left her name out of it. No matter what, I
didn't want her to become involved.''

Gideon was still incredulous over the kind of loyalty
she and Heidi had shown each other. ''Tell me why
she came over.''

''I thought you said you already knew.''

''I have Heidi's version of that night, Dana. Now I
want yours. Two people recalling the same incident tell
it differently. I'm looking for clues that will help me
find out who killed Amy.''

Dana bit her lip, then nodded. ''Earlier that day
Heidi and I had gone out in the rowboat to sunbathe
and finish planning our trip to Mexico. She insisted on

rowing because she said she needed the exercise. I figured she needed an outlet for her anger.''

"Why anger?''

"She was mad at herself for agreeing to go on a blind date. There's a teacher at Mesa Junior who has a brother in the navy. He had come home on leave before shipping out again. She wanted him to meet Heidi because she was convinced they were perfect for each other. She was very insistent, despite Heidi's concerns.'' Dana grimaced. "You know the kind of situation I'm talking about.''

Gideon was afraid he did. He'd suffered through a bad blind date years ago, thanks to a determined colleague.

"Heidi had misgivings, as I said. If she didn't like him, she'd hate to have to turn him down for a second date, maybe hurt his feelings. On the other hand, if he didn't like her, it would make her friend uncomfortable.

"The whole time we were out in the boat, she went back and forth, trying to decide what to do. We never did talk about our trip. Finally I suggested we row to shore. I said jokingly that she might as well agonize in my dad's study while I worked on my paper.

"Heidi apologized for being such a pain and announced she was going back to her apartment. We said goodbye at the pier. Our plan was to get together the next day and go down to the travel office.

"To my surprise, she came by the house later that night all upset because she'd broken her date and now the guy and his sister were both furious at her. She felt horrible about it and asked me to go for a drive with her.

"I told her okay, just give me a few more minutes. At that point she admitted she wasn't fit company for anyone. After telling me she'd call in the morning, she left."

"Let's stop right there. Do you have any idea if Amy was in the house at that time?"

"You mean while Heidi was there?"

"Yes."

"None at all. But later, when Dad told me not to say anything to anyone, it struck me that if the police knew Heidi had been at the house, they'd start probing. I remembered that her fingerprints were on the oar handles."

"But that was her family's rowboat. Those alone wouldn't have connected her to the crime."

"No, but Heidi usually mows the front lawn when her parents are away. Which meant that her fingerprints would have been on the mower and the gas can in their garage."

Gideon could see where this was going. "You were afraid the police might think Heidi helped you set Amy's bedroom on fire."

"Yes. I'm so glad I kept quiet about her. Especially when Mr. Cobb told me what Amy had written in her diaries about Heidi and me."

The diaries.

He'd seen a lot of terrible things in his career, but those diaries were filled with damning revelations and accusations that couldn't be contested because Amy was dead. Intertwined through the passages was a

After we were married and Kevin was born, Max and I were called to testify at a police-brutality trial. It was such a traumatic experience we both left the police department. He ended up with the FBI, and I moved my family out to San Diego, where I went into criminal-investigation work.

"Fay got a job at a stock brokerage here. It didn't take her long to have another affair—with the man she's married to now."

"Gideon!" Heidi was shocked.

"When I met Fay, I think I was in love with love. We were opposites in too many ways, but we were young and we found the differences fascinating. Marriage seemed the next natural step, but it was a mistake from the beginning. Still, I was determined to make it work.

"To cut a long story short, she came home from the office one day and told me she planned to leave me because she was in love with someone else.

"I was stunned. No matter how bad things were, I hadn't believed she'd look for love outside our marriage. I suggested we go for counseling. She refused. At that point I told her she could have her freedom, but I was suing for custody of Kevin.

"That's when she informed me he wasn't my son and I learned about her affair in New York. A DNA test confirmed that I couldn't possibly be the biological father. Of course, that made no difference to my feelings for Kevin.

"I went for some counseling through the department. The psychologist convinced me that a child needs his mother during the formative years, so I ended up asking for liberal visitation rights.

"Kevin loves his mother, but she's worked all these years, leaving him with baby-sitters and nannies. Unfortunately he's never bonded with his stepfather, who's actually a pretty nice guy."

Heidi shook her head. "No wonder Kevin clings to you."

"He's been begging to live with me."

"How does your ex-wife feel about that?"

He let out a deep sigh. "You don't want to know."

"Oh, Gideon…what you've told me makes me more apprehensive than ever. I don't want to add to Kevin's insecurity."

"It's too late for that. This is something he'll have to work through, because there's no way I'm going to give you up. I told you all this so you'd understand Kevin's history and be prepared to help me with him."

As much as Heidi hated to think it, she blamed Gideon's ex-wife to a great extent for fostering this insecurity in her son. A mother could make all the difference in smoothing the way for an ex-spouse in his relationship with his children. Heidi had seen it over and over again at school; she frequently encountered the emotional problems faced by kids from divorced homes. So often, the mother's attitude to her ex was reflected by the children's attitude to him—and it could be a positive and comfortable situation for everyone.

Of course, that mother needed to be unselfish.

That thought brought Heidi right back to the beginning. If Gideon's wife *hadn't* been selfish, she wouldn't have been unfaithful to anyone as wonderful as Gideon. No doubt they'd still be married today.

And if *that* were true, Heidi wouldn't be with him now. She couldn't even imagine that. Not after what they'd shared this evening. Already he'd become as necessary to her as...as breathing.

"Heidi?"

His voice returned her to the present. "Yes?"

"You look tired. I'm not surprised after the shock you received today. I think it's time you were in bed. Tomorrow morning will be soon enough to plan our strategy."

Dana.

For a little while Heidi had been so consumed by thoughts of Gideon, she'd almost forgotten the reason for being here at all.

By tacit agreement they got up from the couch. He clasped her hand and gave her a tour of the rest of the house, Pokey trotting along behind.

To her surprise the living room was at the opposite end of the house. The furnishings were more formal than modern. Gideon let her take a look in each of the three bedrooms off the hall.

"You have a beautiful home," she said. "I like the way it's a mixture of traditional and modern. No clutter. Everything's spotless."

By now they stood outside the guest bedroom.

"I can thank my housekeeper for that."

"Lucky you," she said lightly.

"Lucky me is right."

She didn't know what he meant until he took her in his arms and proceeded to kiss her. Heidi melted against him—until he suddenly drew back. Her hands were still splayed against his chest.

"A little while ago I made you a promise," he whispered. "I intend to keep it."

She couldn't suppress a groan.

"I feel the same way," he said.

It was humiliating to realize he had more strength of will than she did. The last thing she wanted was to let go of him. Slowly, reluctantly, she removed her hands from his chest and backed into the bedroom.

"Good night. I'll see you in the morning." Shutting the door, she leaned against it, too weakened by longing to do anything else.

If Gideon hadn't been the kind of man he was, she would have leaped into the flames just now. Living under the same roof with him was risky—she'd known that when he'd first suggested it, but she'd thought she could handle it.

Who was she kidding?

CHAPTER TEN

POKEY'S WHINING brought Gideon out of a restless sleep. He raised his head to look at his watch. It was five-thirty in the morning, too early for the dog to want out.

Gideon doubted Heidi was awake yet. Maybe someone other than the paperboy had come into the yard.

He shoved the covers aside and got out of bed. Pokey stood on full alert next to the closed door. Curious to know what had disturbed the dog, Gideon shrugged into his bathrobe.

"Come on, boy. Show me what's got you so excited."

As soon as he finished tying his belt, he opened the bedroom door. Pokey bounded down the hall. Gideon could see light from the kitchen end of the house. Since he'd turned everything off before going to bed, he knew Heidi had to be up.

To his surprise he found her fully dressed, sitting on the couch in the family room. She was reading one of the diary pages. Pokey leaned against her legs as she rubbed behind his ears.

"Gideon," she said softly when she saw him enter the room. He liked the way her eyes played over him, as if she couldn't help herself. "I'm so sorry if I woke you."

"You didn't. I've been ready to get up for some time. How did you sleep?" He couldn't resist asking, because she still looked tired. She also looked so damn beautiful it frustrated him all over again that they'd spent the night apart.

"Fine."

Liar.

"Actually that's not true," she admitted. "I tossed and turned for hours trying to make sense of everything. Just a little while ago I realized what was troubling me." Her eyes darted to his once more. "I'm glad you're up. I need to talk to you about it."

With the advent of morning came reality. Gideon resented its intrusion.

"I'll let Pokey out first and feed him. Come on, boy."

Once that was accomplished, he returned to the kitchen. "I'm making coffee. Do you take sugar? Cream?"

"Both," she called out.

As soon as he carried the mugs to the table, she joined him, bringing all the diary pages with her.

"Tell me what's on your mind." He sat down in the chair next to her and handed her the coffee.

She drank a good portion of it. "Mmm, that tastes wonderful. Thank you," she said before putting the mug aside. "I want you to see something." Quickly she found the first page of each diary and spread all six of them out in chronological order.

"According to the first entry, Amy would have been

in seventh grade. But no twelve-year-old wrote this! Look at her handwriting, the level of her vocabulary, then compare it to the five other diaries. I may not be an expert, but I am a teacher and I require my students to keep a portfolio of their work.

"Those who've been with me from seventh through ninth grade reveal some improvement over that time. There are always differences—evidence of growth in maturity and legibility.

"But from the ages of twelve to nineteen, Amy's writing is the same. I don't see that gradual change. There are no spelling errors to speak of. Her grammatical construction is sound. All the volumes show the same degree of development."

He put down his coffee to study them.

She was right!

With the diaries lined up like this, the proof leaped out at him, substantiating a theory of his that had only been in an embryonic stage until now.

Excited by Heidi's insight, he grasped her hand and squeezed it. "Do you know what you've done?"

Her gaze clung to his. "Not really."

"While I was reading the first volume yesterday morning, I got the distinct impression it wasn't a true diary. By the time I'd finished all the volumes, I felt that I'd been reading the rough draft of a cleverly crafted novel or play. Everything seemed to have been orchestrated for one express purpose."

"You mean, to hurt Dana."

He released her hand. "Surely that goes without saying. But there's much more to it than that. What you've just noticed is so vital to this case that without your inspiration, I might not have been able to piece everything together nearly this fast.''

Her eyes widened. ''You mean I've really found something that could help?''

''More than you know. Consider the fact that neither you nor Dana had any idea Amy kept a diary. That, in and of itself, doesn't necessarily mean she *didn't* keep one. But if your recollection is true and you're correct in your assessment of her writing, then it means she wrote all these volumes very recently. What would that tell you?''

''That at the age of nineteen she sat down and reconstructed her past in diary form,'' Heidi said promptly.

''Maybe.''

''Or she could have planned to pass off the diaries as authentic. I know it's a stretch, but perhaps she hoped they'd eventually be made into a film she could star in. Another scenario is that she was consciously writing fiction with the hope of getting it published someday.''

''Those are both possibilities.''

''But you don't believe them any more than I do.''

''How can you tell?''

''The tone of your voice. Your body language.''

His lips twitched. It pleased him no end that she could already read him so well. It meant she'd been studying him, thinking about him.

''You're not going to tell me what your theory is, are you.''

He finished the rest of his coffee. ''Not yet. First we need proof that we're on the right track. As soon as I get dressed, we'll have breakfast, then drive to your house so you can pack and do whatever you have to do.

"By that time we'll be able to make phone calls without waking people up. The first person I want to talk to is Mrs. Winegar, the teacher Amy referred to. The one who gave her the diary."

"I think she made up that name, along with everything else, Gideon."

"If that's true, then the more lies we can prove, the more a real picture of Amy will emerge. Tell me something. When you were younger, did you ever get one of those kits where you paint a picture by number? All the threes were yellow, all the fours were blue, et cetera?"

Heidi nodded.

"Well, that's the way I look at suspects during an investigation. In the beginning, they're a colorless shape waiting to come to life. As I learn about a fact or a memory, I fill in a space. Then I uncover a lie and fill in another space. One lie often leads to another. The picture starts to come together until I gradually arrive at the truth."

Silence followed and her eyes searched his for a moment.

"You just said 'suspects,'" she finally said. "But Amy was the victim!"

Again it gratified him that she was such a quick study; still, he couldn't resist teasing her.

"Now you've disappointed me."

She looked crestfallen. "I don't understand."

"You've broken the first rule Daniel Mcfarlane wrote on your blackboard."

Deciding to let her think about that for a while, Gideon stood up from the table. He put his hands on her shoulders and bent down to kiss the side of her neck. "If you want to start breakfast while I get ready, you won't hear any complaints from me."

Halfway down the hall he heard footsteps behind him. "Gideon…" She followed him into his bedroom and stepped in front of him so he'd have to stop and face her.

"If you're saying what I think you're saying, you believe Amy staged her own death to make it look like Dana murdered her."

"Ms. Ellis? You go to the head of the class."

Her hands flew to her mouth. "Then…then she had to be out of her mind!"

"Maybe she suffered from true mental illness. It's an avenue we're going to explore. We'll also find out if she was a drug user whose world became too distorted for her to behave rationally."

Heidi groaned. "I never thought of drugs. There would've been evidence of that—right?"

It was apparent that Heidi didn't know there'd been no autopsy. Dana and the Turners had done a good job of keeping her uninformed. Gideon decided not to say anything about it just yet.

"They might not be a factor, but we won't rule anything out. Can you arrange a meeting with the Turners today? We'll need all the help they can give us."

"I'll call them right now. They won't have gone to work yet. When they find out you're investigating the case, I know they'll be so thankful they'll do anything they can." She hurried out of the bedroom.

Gideon headed for the shower, anxious to find the proof that would free Dana from prison. The day that happened, her life would begin again. And so would his. However, he wasn't going to complain about the present. Heidi had already spent one night under his roof. Even if she hadn't been in his bed.

SECOND PERIOD at Las Palmas Middle School had already started by the time Heidi and Gideon entered the front office. She and Dana had been students here when it was still a junior high. Except for updated technology, nothing seemed to have changed about the place since.

The secretary looked up from her computer.

"May I help you?"

"I hope so. I'm Heidi Ellis, the teacher from Mesa Junior High who called you about an hour ago trying to locate an English teacher named Mrs. Winegar. This is Detective Poletti with the San Diego criminal-investigations department."

"How do you do," the other woman said. "After you phoned, I asked anyone on staff who came by the office this morning if they recalled the name. Two of the teachers have been here for thirty years. They said they'd never heard of her. I'm sorry."

"Lie number one verified," Gideon whispered as his hand slid up Heidi's back. "What now, Sherlock?"

She could scarcely concentrate with him touching her.

"We appreciate your help. Does the school keep old

yearbooks on file? We'd like to look at a couple of them.''

''I believe Mr. Delgado has them locked in the large storage closet behind his counter. He runs the media center. It's midway down the next hall on your right. I'll tell him you're on your way.''

''Thank you. Oh,'' Heidi said, ''could we have a printout of your current staff with their room assignments? I once went to school here. If it turns out those yearbooks we're looking for are missing, I'd like to be able to talk to the teachers whose names I still recognize.''

''Help yourself from that stack at the end of the counter. We leave them out for parents.''

''Thanks again.''

Gideon moved his hand to her waist as he ushered her out of the office. ''Congratulations,'' he murmured. ''You're starting to think like a detective. I'm impressed.''

''Elementary, my dear Watson,'' she teased, but his compliment brought her great pleasure. ''Any sleuthing skills I've got have been developed by necessity in order to survive my own particular jungle.''

He was still laughing at her remark as they walked into the media center, which was filled with students. The man at the counter waved them over.

''Mr. Delgado?''

''Good morning. The office told me you were on your way. I've pulled out the yearbooks for the past decade. You'd better come into my office to look at them.''

His office was no more than a cubicle, but at least

it was private. He brought in an extra chair and closed the door for them.

Heidi searched through the pile until she found the yearbooks that would have covered Amy's seventh and eighth grades. She handed one to Gideon and took the other. They leafed through them until they located her pictures.

"She and Dana don't bear a strong resemblance to each other," Gideon said.

"No," Heidi agreed. "When you meet the Turners, you'll notice they're blond and kind of short. Dana looks more like her grandmother on her father's side."

"Let's check faculty names against the ones on the printout."

Heidi put the paper between them. After a thorough scrutiny, she said, "I can only find four teachers from either yearbook who are still working here. None are English teachers. I have no idea if any of them even taught her."

Gideon pressed a swift kiss to her lips. "Let's drive to the district office. They can look up her records and print them out for us. We'll also ask for the names of her former teachers."

They thanked Mr. Delgado, then left the building and headed for the education office. Seeing a detective at work was a revelation. All Gideon had to do was flash his credentials and everyone scurried to accommodate his requests. Within the hour they had a list of every teacher who'd taught Amy, including their current teaching status and their schools, if they were still working in the district.

"It looks like her seventh-grade English teacher was a Ms. Ferron. That's not a name I remember."

"According to this, the woman's not working in this district anymore. I'll call headquarters. They'll find her. In the meantime let's go back to Las Palmas and talk to Mr. Finch, the shop teacher. He's the one person who's still there and taught Amy."

They returned to the school, timing their arrival between classes.

When they'd introduced themselves, the older man lifted his safety goggles to get a better look at Gideon's credentials. "Amy Turner, you say? Yes, I remember her. It's a terrible tragedy—being murdered by her own sister."

His comment sent a shudder through Heidi's body. Gideon pulled her closer.

"I'm not at all certain her sister was the culprit, Mr. Finch. That's why we're here asking questions. Tell us your impression of Amy. It could be very important."

"Well..." The other man scratched his head. "She was on the quiet side. Kind of lived in her own world. No friends to speak of in my class, but that's not unusual, considering only a small percentage of girls sign up for shop.

"Amy never caused any trouble. But there was one thing I do recall. Every year before summer recess, the kids make pendulum clocks to give their dads on Father's Day. She did a nice job on hers, but I found it in the room hidden behind some equipment after school closed. That's the only thing about her that stands out in my mind."

"It's exactly the kind of information we need," Gideon assured him. "If I may ask one more question—did you notice anything about her behavior that would lead you to believe she took drugs?"

Mr. Finch shook his head. "No. Generally the kids on drugs have noticeable mood swings. You can spot them right off because they don't handle the machinery and equipment properly when they're under the influence."

At that point the bell rang and the students reappeared. It became impossible to compete with the din of the machines.

Gideon reached out to shake the teacher's hand. "Thank you. You've been a great help."

"Anytime."

They walked slowly out of the school, both of them silent.

"What do you think?" Gideon asked on the way to the car.

"I keep wondering about Amy's warped view of her life. Dr. Turner is such a kind, extraordinary man, who thought the world of his daughters. I never saw him show either one of them anything but love. He would have cherished that clock."

"You and I might know that, but it's obvious from the diaries that jealousy of Dana had a stranglehold on Amy from an early age. With her perception so twisted, I would guess she had serious doubts about her own worth."

"For as long as I can remember, Dana was aware of Amy's sensitivity. She always tried not to hurt her feelings. And she made a real effort to give her encouragement and recognition."

"That probably angered Amy further."

"You're right."

No sooner had he helped her into the car than his cell phone rang. "It's headquarters getting back to me."

Heidi glanced at her watch. The Turners were expecting them at one. That gave them two hours to track down the English teacher. While she waited, she noticed Gideon jotting a number on his notepad.

"Barbara Ferron is now Barbara Lowell. This is a home phone number. Let's hope she's there."

He punched in the digits, and to her relief he began talking to someone. The next thing she knew, she heard him say they'd be there shortly.

His face broke out in a satisfied smile as he turned off his phone and started the car. "The Lowells now have two children. She hasn't taught since she left Las Palmas six years ago. They recently moved into a new block of condos in City Heights. It shouldn't take us long to get there."

"Oh, Gideon..."

He reached for her hand. "I know what you're feeling. When you've got a strong hunch about a case, you're impatient for everything to fall into place."

She squeezed his fingers, then released them. "I can see how you could lose yourself in chasing down leads."

He nodded. "For some of the guys it becomes an addiction. It can play havoc with marriage and family life. Last year I worked on a special task force with Max. It cut down on the time I could spend with Kevin. I suspect that's contributed to the problems he's having now. As a result, I vowed I'd never put duty before family again."

She bowed her head. "In Kevin's eyes, your spending time with me is as threatening to him as any task force."

Gideon placed his hand on her thigh. The touch sent a current of desire through her. "We'll just keep including him and reassuring him until the threat is gone."

That was easier said than done, but she'd fallen under Gideon's spell and *wanted* to believe him. When they were within touching distance, anything seemed possible.

She couldn't lie to herself any longer. She was in love with him. No matter what the future held, she knew with certainty that there could never be anyone else.

THE LIVING ROOM of Barbara Lowell's small condo looked like an advertisement for baby paraphernalia. She had a cute two-year-old who clung to the webbing of the playpen, watching them. But Gideon's eyes were drawn over and over to the sight of Heidi as she cradled the woman's nine-month-old infant in her arms. It made him hunger for things he hadn't allowed himself to think about in years.

The woman, who appeared to be in her early thirties, sat down on a chair opposite the couch.

"Detective Poletti? I have to tell you that when you mentioned Amy Turner's name, it really gave me a jolt."

"Because of her murder?"

"That, too, of course, but I was thinking more of the year I taught her. It was my first—and only—teaching experience. Seasoned teachers told me it would be tough. With a student like Amy, I soon learned they weren't exaggerating.

"To be honest, I was glad to get married and move to Texas with Gary. We've only been back here since July. Even when my kids are older, I'm not sure I'll return to teaching." She sighed. "Anyway, as I said, I only taught one year, so the memories are still pretty vivid."

"Tell us what you remember about Amy."

"I believe she was a very troubled girl."

"In what way?"

"As far as I could tell, she had virtually no self-esteem. It permeated her writing. The very first assignment she handed in actually alarmed me. I thought it might be a joke. Because I was so new to teaching, I feared I couldn't see it for what it really was, so I showed it to the school psychologist.

"She agreed Amy might have serious emotional problems, but one sample wasn't enough to raise a red flag. She might be trying to shock me, or perhaps it was a cry for attention. I agreed both reasons could apply in her case.

"The psychologist told me to watch for more of the same. If a pattern developed, then I should come to her again."

"What was the assignment?"

"I asked the students to write a story about themselves that would be put in a time capsule to be read fifty years from now. I emphasized that the only history available to people half a century later would be what they gleaned from the kids' stories. Therefore, the students needed to reveal the essence and richness of their lives and culture.''

· ''What did she write?''

''She handed in a short paragraph, badly written, that basically said life sucks and her family hates her.'' Gideon exchanged glances with Heidi. ''I corrected the papers and handed them back. On Amy's paper I wrote a note, asking her to see me after school.

''I told her she'd missed the point of the assignment, and I insisted she try again. In an effort to encourage her, I gave her some examples to study. Her second attempt was no improvement, and for the rest of the year she handed in mostly failing assignments that were very dark in content.

''Neither of her parents could come to the conferences, but we talked on the phone, which was fine. They said they'd noticed a change in her over the summer and had put her in private counseling. Knowing the Turners were trying to get on top of the problem, I felt relieved. But nothing ever really changed.''

The baby started to fuss. As Heidi handed her back to the mother, she said, ''By any chance did you require your students to keep a journal?''

''No. The English department had dropped that project from the curriculum the year before I was hired.''

''From an academic standpoint, how would you judge Amy's English?''

''The first thing the psychologist and I did was check SAT scores. Hers were below average. Her writing resembled a fifth-grader's. But that was true for a number of the students.''

"What was she like socially?"

"Amy was reserved, but she wasn't a complete loner."

"Mrs. Lowell," Gideon interjected, "did you ever give her a set of six pocket-size diaries, suggesting she use them to record her private thoughts?"

"No." She shook her head. "Why do you ask?"

"Because the police found six diaries of hers, which the prosecution leaned on heavily in order to put her sister in prison. The first diary dates back to the year you were teaching at Las Palmas. The beginning paragraph states that Mrs. Winegar, her English teacher, gave her the diary she was writing in."

"Mrs. Winegar—"

"Does that name ring a bell?"

"Yes! Just a minute."

Carrying the baby, she hurried out of the room and returned a moment later. On her left hand she wore a large puppet of a very prim-looking Victorian spinster.

"*This* is Mrs. Winegar. She knows her grammar. When she hears one of the students make a mistake in class like 'Lay down,' she breaks in and says, 'You lay an egg, but you lie down.'"

Heidi and Gideon made eye contact. He got to his feet.

"I'm investigating this case on behalf of Dana Turner, Amy's sister. Dana's attorney, John Cobb, will be getting in touch with you to take a deposition. He might even decide to put you on the witness stand when this case goes to court again. Would you agree to that?''

"Of course."

"Thank you for your time, Mrs. Lowell. You've been more helpful than you know. We'll let ourselves out."

Gideon placed his arm around Heidi's shoulders as they walked to the car. "Remember that blank picture?" She nodded. "Between Mr. Finch and Mrs. Lowell, all the ones and twos have been filled in. Now we're going to work on the threes. We've still got an hour before we have to meet with Dana's parents. That gives us enough time to run by headquarters."

"What are we going to do there?"

"I'll show you." He opened the back door to retrieve the photocopy of the first diary. When Heidi had secured her seat belt, he handed it to her.

"Look on the inside front cover page. What do you see?" Closing the door, he went around to his side to get behind the wheel. She glanced over at him with a puzzled expression.

"It says Millward Paper Products. Los Angeles, California. I don't see wha— Oh!" she interrupted herself. "You want to find out if this diary was even on the market seven years ago!"

After he'd merged with the traffic, he smiled at her. "You're a natural at this."

"Hardly," she said with a self-deprecating laugh. "I wouldn't have thought of it in a million years, without your hint. Thank heaven for a detective like you who can see what other people can't."

Gideon's hands tightened on the steering wheel.

"For Dana's sake, let's hope that's true. However, I don't think we should count on too much where the diaries are concerned.

"It would be nice to establish that they weren't available for purchase seven years ago, but it's entirely possible that particular line has been around for a decades." When he heard her sigh, he said, "Don't worry. A good handwriting expert can tell us a lot. And the forensics department has methods of identifying the age of paper and ink."

She nodded. After a minute she murmured, "The puppet obviously captured Amy's imagination."

"Amy may have had low SAT scores, but it didn't mean her mind wasn't razor-sharp. That's often the case with suspects who have a dark side to their natures. Like I said earlier, she managed to weave enough truth among her lies to put a lethal weapon in Ron Jenke's hands."

"Have you ever met him?"

"Yes. He and I have been in the courtroom together many times."

"How do you think he'll react when he finds out Dana's case is going to be reopened?"

"Unless I've got critical evidence, he'll fight to prevent it."

"That's horrible!"

"He has a reputation to protect."

"But we're talking about Dana's *life!* If she was *his* client—"

"None of it matters, Heidi. Once our evidence is lined up, there won't be anything Jenke can do to stop us."

He could feel her eyes on him. "You really believe she committed suicide?"

"What better way to go out of this life and make certain her nemesis would suffer? Amy could have hidden her diaries anywhere, but she purposely put them in Dana's closet before setting fire to her own bedroom. Amy knew those words would condemn Dana. She had to ensure they weren't destroyed."

"But to set her own room on fire, knowing she'd die… Where was her will to live?"

"Probably diminished by drugs, although I have no actual proof of that yet. When Dana was telling me about their physical fight, she said Amy had incredible strength. Enough to pull her to the floor and beat her."

Heidi groaned quietly, as though this was too painful to bear.

"If you've ever watched someone high on hallucinogens, you'd see a person whose world is totally distorted. There was a case last month of a college student who took some LSD and thought a monster had come into his hotel room.

"According to witnesses, he tried to push it out the window, which was sealed shut. So he broke the glass with his bare hands and fell twenty stories to his death."

"I remember hearing about that on the news. It was awful."

"The point is, Amy may have planned the whole scenario, but it probably took drugs to help her act on it."

"How could we find out? I'm afraid her friends would never tell us."

"They might if they realized the case was going back to court and they could be named accessories to a murder."

He heard her sharp intake of breath. "Do you think it's possible they knew what Amy was planning and lied for her on the witness stand?"

"The thought's crossed my mind. If they *were* a party to any of it, we're sure as hell going to find out!"

Before long they'd arrived back at headquarters. "Come on. I'll take you down to the archives to see the diaries."

"I've never been here before. It's kind of scary, but exciting, too."

He smiled. "Kevin said the same thing the first time I brought him with me. Have no fear. This place has been my home away from home for years now."

Once they got out of the car in the underground parking, he took her hand and held on tightly. It was important she see where he worked. He wanted her to know everything about him.

CHAPTER ELEVEN

"YOU TWO CAN USE cubicle D."

"Thanks, Ben."

Gideon ushered Heidi into the little room. She stared in horror at the innocent-looking pile of books he put on the table. It took a minute before she could find the courage to examine them.

"What?" he demanded when she shook her head.

"Amy used every conceivable color of ink to fill these volumes." She lifted her head to gaze at him. "Thank God you thought to have photocopies made first," she said. "In black and white it was easy to see the uniformity of her writing. But with all these colors, I doubt I would even have noticed."

"That's what Amy was counting on. In fact, she was so clever, not even Cobb's expert witness caught it." He caressed her cheek with his index finger. "When Dana's free, she'll have you to thank for it."

Heidi's eyes filled. "None of this would be possible without you," she whispered.

His chest rose and fell visibly. "I only hope my theory's correct. I don't like the idea of Dana spending time behind bars any more than you do. Now, let's check out this paper company."

He pulled out his cell phone and rang information,

requesting the number of Millward Paper Products in Los Angeles. He wrote down a number and punched it in, but then was put on hold several times. When he could finally make an inquiry about the diary, she found herself holding her breath.

Reaching for one of the volumes, he read aloud the design number from the inside cover. Eventually she heard him ask the person on the other end if he or she would testify to that in a court of law. Her blood pounded in her ears.

Unable to remain seated any longer, she jumped to her feet. Her action caught Gideon's attention. His blue eyes seemed to come alive as he turned off the phone.

"You can start filling in all the threes in our picture." He stood up and gathered the diaries from the table. "This happens to be a new line of diaries put out on the market a year ago February for a Valentine's Day promotion."

"Gideon…"

His mouth formed a half smile. "This brings us a little closer to establishing my premise that every move on Amy's part was premeditated. When our picture's complete, we'll be ready to sit down with Mr. Cobb.

"Let's go." He opened the door for her. "I'm anxious to meet with the Turners and walk around the crime scene."

"I can't wait for them to meet you! Next to my parents, they're my favorite people. To be honest, I don't know how they've survived this long. Since Amy's death, life for them has turned into the ultimate endurance test."

"I imagine their need to help and support Dana is what keeps them going," he said.

Heidi nodded vigorously. "Yes. And what you're doing will make such a difference to them."

She paused. "The only thing I've told them is that you've begun another investigation of the case on behalf of my parents and me. When they hear what you have to say, it's going to transform their world."

TRANSFORM THEIR WORLD

During the drive to Mission Bay, those words went around Gideon's head like a mantra. Heidi's faith in him was humbling. More than ever he wanted to be all things to her. His determination to effect Dana's release had become his number-one priority.

A half hour later Heidi pointed out her parents' house next door as they entered the Turners' driveway. She introduced him to Dana's mother and father. They greeted Heidi like family and welcomed him with genuine graciousness. Yet they looked and acted like war victims still in shock. Who could blame them?

Mrs. Turner dispensed with formality and insisted Gideon call them Christine and Ed. She seemed intent on serving them lunch first. That was just as well, because it gave him the opportunity to find out what charming, intelligent people they were.

Dana's mother taught English literature at the state university; her husband was a renowned astronomer. The two of them were well suited and seemed devoted to each other.

Lunch was served in the dining room of their spacious home. Large picture windows stretching across the back of the house faced the bay, offering a breathtaking view of the water. Gideon wished he didn't have life-and-death matters on his mind so he could appreciate it better.

After finishing his dessert, he decided to plunge in with his theory. No point in leading up to it gently, he felt—best to simply state it and go on from there. From the beginning the Turners had believed in Dana's innocence—but they were still under the illusion that Amy's killer was out there somewhere.

What he had to tell them was going to hurt them in ways they hadn't imagined. However, if it meant Dana could be restored to them, he was sure their joy in getting her back would overshadow that pain.

"Quite a bit has happened since Heidi first came to my criminology class. For one thing, I'm convinced Dana is innocent of any wrongdoing. But I'm just as convinced that no one murdered Amy."

Their heads lifted a little higher in surprise.

"It's my belief she planned her own suicide to make it appear that Dana murdered her," he said bluntly.

"Suicide!" Christine gasped. Her husband shot Gideon a look of disbelief.

"This morning Heidi and I spoke with two of Amy's teachers from seventh grade. Both corroborated my belief that your daughter was a troubled girl even back then.

"I have no idea how long she thought about taking her own life. Maybe it was months, maybe years. We do know the diaries reveal a pathological jealousy of Dana. We also know something else about the diaries, thanks to Heidi."

He turned his head in her direction. "You tell them."

For the next few minutes, Heidi explained what they'd discovered from looking at the photocopies. Then she told them what the manufacturer had said about the date the diaries were put on the market.

"So you see, those diaries aren't the real thing. Amy couldn't have written in them before Valentine's Day of last year, because that design didn't exist.

"She made up lie after lie, knowing full well she wouldn't be around for anyone to question what she wrote. To make sure the police found them, she hid all six volumes in Dana's closet. Amy must've figured that would cast even more suspicion on her sister, who had no knowledge of the diaries' existence."

After a long silence Christine said, "I'd never seen her with a diary." Tears ran down her face. "Our daughter was so sick, Ed."

"If I can interject..." Gideon spoke up. "When I went to the prison, something Dana told me about Amy's strength the night of her death led me to believe she might have been on drugs. They could have helped her cross the line into irrational behavior."

Christine shook her head. "I wasn't aware she took drugs. Did you ever suspect?" she asked her husband.

"No. But I was never comfortable with the kind of company she kept."

"Neither was I. Those two friends of hers weren't like normal girls. Not happy and bright."

Gideon sat back in his chair. "I intend to get the information I need out of them. But I also want the best coroner I know to perform an autopsy on Amy."

Heidi stared at him. "There *wasn't* one?" she asked incredulously.

"No." He looked at the Turners. "One of the reasons I'm here today is to obtain your permission for her body to be exhumed."

A cry burst out of Christine and she buried her face in her hands. Ed went over to comfort his wife.

"I know how grim that sounds," Gideon commiserated. "Dana told me none of you wanted to have it done, but I believe it's necessary in order to get at the truth. The coroner's report said she died from smoke inhalation. That was determined as a result of a postmortem blood test, which revealed toxic levels of carbon monoxide.

"That, plus the physical evidence of a struggle, gave Jenke his ironclad case. And then he went to trial armed with those diaries. Not surprisingly the jury bought his arguments.

"But I've investigated many arson murders. After an autopsy's been performed, you'd be surprised how often it's discovered that death was attributable to another cause."

Dr. Turner's face was drawn. "Neither the police nor the coroner insisted on it, since cause of death seemed so clear-cut. John Cobb urged us to have it done, but it didn't seem right at the time."

"Unfortunately smoke inhalation is a great masker of truth," Gideon continued. "Only an autopsy will reveal secrets—if there are any."

Christine wiped her eyes. "So what you're saying is, it's possible she might have died from an overdose of drugs before the smoke got to her."

"That's right."

Dr. Turner straightened. "You make a lot of sense, Gideon. But if Amy was on drugs that night, would there still be traces in her body after almost a year?"

"That depends on several factors."

"Like what?" Christine whispered.

"How well she was embalmed—the condition of her grave."

Just hearing the words made the older woman groan.

"Not every drug will necessarily show up. But even if I'm wrong about drugs, maybe an autopsy will yield other information of which we're not aware."

She stared at her husband through her tears. "We have to do it for Dana's sake!"

"I agree, honey."

Relief swept over Gideon. "Good. Where's she buried?"

"Mount Hope City Cemetery."

"I'll get an exhumation order through the police department before the day is out. Now...there's something else.

"I'm not a psychiatrist, but I'm sure if we consulted one, he or she would come up with some medical term that would apply to Amy's mental problems. Sometime this week I'd like to talk to the person you sent her to for counseling in seventh grade."

"I remember," Christine said. "It was the Bay Shore adolescent psychiatric unit. Dr. Siricca."

"Would you mind calling to find out if that doctor's still there?"

"I'll do it right now."

As she hurried from the room, Ed said, "I know you

wanted to view the crime scene. Let me show you where the bedrooms are. Amy's room is between ours and Dana's. Of course, it's been remodeled.''

Gideon and Heidi both rose from the table. With his arm around her shoulders, they followed Dr. Turner through the hallway to the other side of the house. Amy's room was a nice size. Sunny. Very feminine.

''The night she died Christine and I had been to a faculty dinner. On our return, we opened the front door and smelled smoke. We discovered it coming from this bedroom. We later learned that all the smoke alarms had been disabled.'' He paused, eyes lowered.

''When we opened the door,'' he continued, ''the smoke was overpowering. Amy lay facedown near the door. The far wall, the bed and the floor around it were on fire.

''We dragged her into the hall, then I picked her up and carried her outside. Christine called the fire department. They were here within a couple of minutes, but it was too late for our Amy.''

Heidi left Gideon's side to comfort Dr. Turner. While the older man wept, Gideon walked down the hall to get a look at Dana's bedroom.

If the Turners hadn't arrived home when they did, this end of the house would have been engulfed in flames, destroying the diaries. Amy had clearly planned everything down to the last detail.

A moment later he found the others in the living room. As soon as Christine saw Gideon enter, she said, ''I just talked to Dr. Siricca. You can go by the hospital anytime after three-thirty this afternoon and she'll be willing to talk to you.''

"Thank you."

He sat down beside Heidi on the sofa and reached for her hand. The eagerness with which she clasped his told him he wasn't the only one looking forward to this evening, when they could be alone. But in the meantime, there were still questions to ask.

"Tell me something, Ed," Gideon began. "The last entry in the diary indicated that Amy planned to run away where no one could find her. She said she was going to use the tuition money you gave her for the summer quarter. When did you do that?"

Dr. Turner lurched in the chair. "I never got the chance to give it to her!"

"The lies in that diary keep stacking up," Gideon murmured.

"On the day she died, she phoned me at the observatory around lunch to ask me if she could have her tuition money to pay her summer fees. I told her I was meeting her mother at a faculty dinner that evening and wouldn't be home until after that. I'd write out a check for her then."

"How do you suppose she knew Dana would be at the house that evening when it was still exam week at Caltech?"

"I can answer that," Christine said. "Dana phoned me at the university that morning to let me know she was on her way home. She'd decided to finish her term paper at our house.

"Midmorning, Amy called me at work to find out if I had her tuition check. I told her she'd have to speak to her father. Before we hung up, I mentioned that Dana would be home shortly."

The older woman struggled for control. "Things had never been good between them. I thought I'd better warn Amy, who'd had the run of the house for a while, that her sister would be arriving. Now I realize I'm the one who—" She couldn't go on and broke down sobbing.

"Don't blame yourself," Gideon said. "Amy was determined to carry through with her plan. If not that night, then another. Since we know she didn't plan to use that money to pay for tuition or run away, it means she needed it for something else."

"Like drugs," Ed suggested in a faint voice.

Gideon nodded. "If she'd run out of her supply and had no money to buy more, it's understandable she'd turn to you. Do you know if she called you from your house?"

Neither parent remembered.

"It doesn't matter. I'd like you to request a copy of your phone bills from February through June of last year."

"You want Amy's cell-phone bills, too?"

"Everything. Try to get them today if you can."

"We will. Is there anything else?"

"Yes. When the police arrived at the house that night and began their investigation, one of the officers went through Dana's purse. He found a receipt with Dana's signature for two gallons of gas from Lyle's Gas Station.

"It was dated the same day Amy died. I noticed she charged it to Lyle's, instead of using a credit card."

Dr. Turner nodded. "Lyle's has been there for ages. I started a charge account with them years ago and it just stayed that way. At the end of every month, I drive over there and pay the bill.''

"Does your family have the same privilege?"

"Yes."

"So Dana and Amy could fill up anytime they wanted and just charge it?"

"That's right."

Gideon's mind shot ahead to more possibilities. "On our way to the hospital, we'll drop by Lyle's. I'd like to talk to the attendant who waited on Dana."

"I'll show you the way," Heidi murmured. "Our family goes there, too. It's three blocks from here."

"We'd better leave now. There's still a lot to do before this day is over." He got up and drew Heidi to her feet. "Thank you for the delicious lunch, Christine. It's been a pleasure meeting you. If I have anything to say about this case, your daughter's going to be a free woman before too much longer."

The older woman rushed forward and threw her arms around him. As soon as she let him go, Ed clasped Gideon's hand in a heartfelt shake. "We'll never be able to thank you enough for what you're doing."

Gideon looked down at the beautiful redhead by his side. "It's my pleasure, believe me. Oh, before we leave, I need the most current pictures of Dana and Amy you have."

"Right here." Christine hurried to the fireplace and brought him two five-by-seven photos.

He studied their pictures. "These will do fine. I'll return them in a few days. Thanks again."

The Turners walked them out to the car.

"I'll drive," Heidi whispered. "Then you can make your call about…about getting Amy's body exhumed."

He gave her waist a confirming squeeze.

When the Turners had waved them off, she backed the car into the street. Once they were on their way, she said, "Dana's a very methodical person, Gideon. She would've made sure she had enough gas to drive all the way from Pasadena. I can't imagine her stopping for a couple of gallons when she was just three blocks from home.

"Even if she did, it would've been for her car, not the mower. Amy probably took an empty gas can with her and forged Dana's name."

"My feelings exactly. The person who waited on her signed the slip with the initials J. V. Do they belong to a name that sounds familiar?"

Her brows met in a delicate frown. "No. I know all the people who work there on a regular basis. It was probably a teenager or college guy hired as part-time help."

Gideon took out his cell phone to call Lieutenant Rodman, who could start the process leading to exhumation and autopsy. While he waited for Rodman to come on the line, he gazed at the woman in the driver's seat. He realized she'd changed his world, changed *him*, until he barely knew himself anymore.

For the past twenty-four hours they'd been together on and off the job. He intended to keep it that way.

TWO HOURS LATER Gideon, carrying Heidi's suitcase, ushered her through the back door of his house. Pokey greeted them in the kitchen. Then Gideon reached for Heidi.

"This is the part I've been waiting for all day. Come here," he said in a husky whisper.

With an eagerness that would make her blush when she recalled it later, Heidi curved into his hard length and met the intensity of his kiss.

Last night had been a time of exploration while they became better acquainted. Tonight she felt as if they'd known each other in another life. Being together all day without having the privacy she craved had ignited her desire to fever pitch.

His body trembled. "Do you have any idea how much I want you?" And then his mouth closed over hers.

The next thing she knew, he'd picked her up in his arms and started down the hall.

"I told you I'd never come into your room without an invitation. But I didn't make any rules about you entering mine."

If felt as though her heart streamed into his as he carried her over the threshold. Then they were on his bed and all coherent thought ceased. Exploding with need, she moved closer to him, hungry for all the things he made her feel.

Suddenly she heard barking from the family room. "Dad? Where are you?"

Kevin.

They both groaned, and Gideon tore his mouth from hers. "I don't believe it. He must have come on the bus."

"Dad?" The boy's voice had grown louder.

Heidi rolled out of Gideon's grasp and jumped off the bed, straightening her skirt and blouse.

"Just a minute, son." Gideon tucked the tail of his shirt into the waistband of his chinos. "I'll be right out."

"Don't let him know I'm here," she begged.

"He'll have seen your suitcase in the kitchen. Don't you realize this moment was inevitable?" He opened the bedroom door.

She shook her head. "I don't want to compound the hurt he's already feeling."

"He has to deal with the fact that I have a life. Come on. Whatever the problem is, we'll face him together."

There was no way out of this, but she could hardly bear to see the pain that would flash in Kevin's eyes.

As they walked down the hall, he reached for her hand and refused to let go. But when they entered the family room, it was Gideon who froze in place.

Seated on the couch next to Kevin was an attractive blond woman in her midthirties. Fashionably dressed in a fawn-colored suede suit, she'd crossed her long legs in a way that emphasized their elegance. The resemblance between mother and son was quite remarkable. She ignored the dog, who'd jumped into Kevin's lap and was licking him.

"Hello, Gideon. I'm sure you're surprised to see me, but I didn't think you'd mind my coming in with Kevin when you hear what I have to say."

Her brown eyes swerved to Heidi, looking her up and down as if she were simply a curiosity.

"Since Gideon hasn't bothered to introduce us, I guess it's up to me. I'm Fay Doctorman, Kevin's mother. He told me his father's girlfriend had red hair. I don't suppose there could be two women like you in his life, so you must be Heidi.''

"That's right. How do you do?''

"You're even younger than I thought.''

Gideon's face was hard, his eyes narrowed. Heidi shivered; she'd had no idea he could look like that. His fingers had tightened around hers.

"Heidi? If you don't mind starting those burgers we're making for dinner, I'll talk to Kevin and his mother in the living room. We won't be long." He released her hand. "Let's go, everybody.''

Kevin's mother swept out, wearing a confident smile. As soon as they'd all gone to the other end of the house, Heidi hurried into the kitchen and reached for her purse. She used her cell phone to call for a taxi, then picked up her suitcase and quietly left Gideon's through the back door.

She knew how her disappearance would look to him. He'd assume his ex-wife's intimidation tactics had worked. But nothing could be further from the truth. Kevin didn't deserve to be in the middle of a confrontation his mother had started.

Heidi felt that removing herself from the scene meant that further unpleasantness could be avoided. She'd been around enough divorced parents who came to school nights bringing new lovers or spouses. The immature couples goaded each other, trying to inflict more pain, but in the end it was the children who got hurt. They were the ones who lost out on the divorce battleground. Heidi refused to be part of it.

As she stood in front of the neighbor's house waiting

for her cab, she decided she was glad Gideon's ex-wife had burst in on them like that. It was the warning Heidi had needed.

There were too many things that still had to be resolved before she got any more involved with Gideon. She'd been wrong to stay at his house. No matter how much she loved him, the last thing she wanted to do was alienate his son. Heidi had no idea if Kevin knew his mother had been unfaithful to Gideon. But whatever he understood about his parents' marriage, Heidi wanted Kevin's trust and respect. Otherwise, she and his father could never have a future together.

As soon as she saw the taxi turn the corner, she expelled the breath she'd been holding. Using her free hand to wave, she ran toward it, eager to be gone before Gideon discovered she was missing.

WHILE KEVIN PLAYED with Pokey in his bedroom, Gideon stared down at Fay, doubting she recognized this monumental moment for what it was.

Ever since he'd learned that Kevin wasn't his biological son, he'd allowed her to manipulate him for the sake of their son's happiness. Over the years he'd let her hold all the cards because he'd chosen not to create any unnecessary tension for his boy.

Tonight was yet another of her attempts to manipulate, this time because she was angry with Gideon for falling in love with someone else.

Fay hadn't expected it to happen. In truth, neither had Gideon.

His ex-wife might have given him up years ago, but she wasn't about to relinquish him to anyone else without making things as difficult as possible. Especially now that she'd met Heidi, a much younger and more beautiful enemy than Fay had envisioned.

"What's taking you so long to answer me?" she said coldly. "I thought you couldn't wait for the day Kevin came to live with you. Now that I've told you he can, why aren't you more excited about it?"

His jaw hardened. "Does Kevin know you brought him to my house because you've suddenly made a decision that could change all our lives forever?"

"Don't be so dramatic, Gideon. Of course he doesn't know."

No, of course not.

Because you don't mean one word of what you're saying. You only barged in here because you were dying to get a good look at Heidi, and you hoped to cause trouble for us.

"I told him I needed to talk to you about something important. He's always thrilled with any opportunity to see you. That is, until just now, when he let us inside with his key and discovered your latest lover in residence. I don't think even he realized how far things have already gone."

Gideon's eyes closed tightly for a moment. After the episode at the hospital, she knew the pain their son was in. Yet she hadn't considered his fragile feelings when she'd brought him over. Without counting the cost, she'd driven Kevin here unannounced in hopes of catching him and Heidi together.

His ex-wife's selfishness had always been repulsive to him, but this time it had caused her to make a fatal mistake. Fay was so certain of Gideon. Now that there was a woman in his life, she assumed he wouldn't take her up on her offer.

Wheeling around, he headed straight for Kevin's bedroom. His son lay on the bed next to Pokey, playing one of his video games. When he saw Gideon, he turned it off and sat up with an anxious look on his face.

"What's wrong, Dad?"

"Not a thing. Your mom's decided you can come and live with me if you want."

Kevin stared at him as if he hadn't heard correctly. "You mean it?" he cried softly. "She really said I could?" Excitement had sent his voice into a higher range.

"Go on into the living room. She'll tell you herself."

He threw himself at Gideon, giving him a bear hug. In the next instant he'd begun to sob. When he finally lifted his head, his face glistened with tears of joy. Then he shot out the door with Pokey in pursuit.

"Mom!" he yelled at the top of his lungs. "Dad says you're going to let me live with him! Oh, Mom— I love you so much!"

Gideon followed at a slower pace. There was no sound from Fay. The horses were out of the barn now, he thought wryly.

For once in her life, she was speechless.

"I'll come and see you all the time and have sleepovers with you, Mom. I promise. Thanks, Mom! Thanks! You're the best!" The happiness he displayed matched Gideon's. He'd wanted his son with him for so long.

"Pokey." He hugged the dog. "We're going to be together every morning and every day after school. And…and every night."

As soon as Fay saw Gideon in the entrance, she stood up, her body trembling with rage. She darted him a venomous glance before leveling her gaze on Kevin.

"I'm afraid I'm going to have to change my mind, Kevin. I had no idea your father was living with someone else."

Ready for that salvo, he backed his son into his arms. "Heidi's not living with me yet. I've already explained to Kevin that I'll only live with a woman if she's my wife.

"As it happens, Heidi and I have both taken time off from our jobs this week to see if we can come up with enough evidence to free her friend from prison. For the sake of convenience, she's staying in the guest bedroom. But Kevin knows he and I are a team forever."

It was up to his son now. It *had* to be his choice, otherwise the change in custody wouldn't work.

"I want to stay with Dad."

Once again Fay had miscalculated.

Elation swept through Gideon. No matter how hard it was for Kevin to accept Heidi, he hadn't let that get in the way of his desire to live with Gideon. Progress had finally been made.

"I'll tell you what, son. Since this will be a big change for everyone, why don't you go on home with your mom and spend tonight with her? You both need time to figure out a schedule that'll work for everyone.

"Tomorrow after school I'll come by the house for you so we can bring some of your stuff over here."

Thankfully he got no argument from Kevin. But the glitter in Fay's eyes alarmed him.

"I have a better idea," she said coldly. "Why don't we let Kevin stay here tonight? The two of you have things to talk about—like the fact that you're not his real father."

CHAPTER TWELVE

THE FRONT DOOR slammed shut. Pokey barked in reaction.

As Kevin turned to Gideon for an explanation, pained confusion was mirrored in his brown eyes.

Fay had done her best to wreak emotional destruction on everyone under Gideon's roof. The carnage had started with Heidi and now it lay strewn from one end of the house to the other. But in her desperate attempt to turn Kevin against him, she might have done the one thing to alienate herself from their son. He was no longer a child. He deserved to know the truth.

"Your mother's right," Gideon said softly. "We do need to talk."

"What did Mom mean about you not being my real dad?"

He put a hand on Kevin's shoulder and walked him over to the couch, where they could sit down.

"Didn't you once tell me your friend Brad Hillyard was adopted?"

"Yeah."

"Does he consider Mr. and Mrs. Hillyard his real parents?"

"Sure." There was a silence while Kevin turned everything over in his mind. "Did you and Mom adopt me?"

"No. We're your real parents, Kevin, and you're our real son. I waited nine months for you to be born. I was there at your delivery. I got to hold and kiss you before your mom did. What she meant was, I'm not the man who made her pregnant."

He blinked as the news sank in. "How come you didn't tell me before?"

"Your mother wanted to tell you when she was ready and felt you could handle the truth. I guess that's up to me now."

Kevin bowed his head. "Did she have an affair?"

Gideon drew a deep breath. "Your mother continued to see another man after she got engaged to me. I didn't know about it until long after we'd moved from New York and you'd turned three years old. About that time she met Frank and asked me for a divorce.

"I knew our marriage hadn't been the greatest, but I hated to see it break up. I told her I wanted custody of you, and that was the moment I learned about the other man—who doesn't know he fathered a child. But the judge declared that you were *my* son, which you are, and granted me liberal visitation rights."

A hand reached out to grasp Gideon's. "I'm glad he did."

"So am I, Kevin." He pulled him into his arms for a hug.

"I always wondered why I didn't look like you."

He cast loving eyes on his son. "You look so much like your mother, I never questioned it. Make no mistake, Kevin. Your mother adores you. In fact, it's a testament to her love that she's finally agreed to let you live with me. Deep down she wants what you want, even if she sounded angry when she left the house a minute ago.''

That part was a lie, but Gideon had no desire to paint a bad picture of Fay. One day, when he was older, Kevin would figure out certain things for himself.

''Remember, she's lived with you and loved you since the day you were born. She's going to miss you very much. To help her, you'll have to visit her a lot from now on to make her realize you love her as much as ever, to prove that nothing's changed.''

''I know.''

''In case you'd forgotten…she lost her parents at a very young age and was taken in by an older aunt who had enough on her hands raising her own four children.

''While your mom was growing up, she suffered insecurities you and I don't know anything about. She's found happiness with Frank. Promise me you won't judge her for a mistake she made fifteen years ago.''

It seemed like an eternity before Kevin said, ''I promise.''

Gideon's eyes filled. ''Do you have any idea what a wonderful son you are? I'm the luckiest father on earth.''

Kevin sniffed, then turned to Gideon. ''I'm sorry we came in the house without ringing the bell. Mom said she wanted to surprise you.''

''I'd say she did a good job of that.'' As for Heidi…

Anxious to talk to her, Gideon got up from the couch. ''Let's check on dinner. Heidi was going to start it, but I can't smell anything.''

They went into the kitchen. When Gideon couldn't see her suitcase, let alone any sign of her, he wasn't surprised, but his heart plunged to his feet.

"I guess she left."

"You're right, Kevin. She's gone."

Heidi must have been shocked that his ex-wife would be that audacious and cruel. He closed his eyes for one brief moment. Knowing Heidi, she was embarrassed to have been caught in the middle of a family problem. It was exactly like her to do everything in her power to avoid coming between him and Kevin.

His son eyed him glumly. "Are you going over to her apartment now?"

Gideon heaved a sigh. "No. I don't even know if she'd be there. Furthermore, I don't want to leave you. I'll get in touch with her later."

Kevin perked up. "Can we take Pokey for a run before we fix dinner?"

"Sure. Let me go put on my running shoes and I'll catch up with you."

"Okay."

When boy and dog had slammed out the back door, Gideon turned sharply away to reach for the phone. Fortunately, he now had Heidi's cell-phone number. Unless she'd turned it off, he'd be able to reach her anywhere.

"JUST A MINUTE, Mom. Someone's on call waiting."

Please be Gideon.

She pressed the flash button. "Hello?"

"Heidi?"

"Hi," she said, relieved.

"Thank God you answered." He sounded as emotional as she felt.

"Just a minute, Gideon. I'm on a call with my mother. Let me say goodbye to her."

"If you need to talk to her longer, phone me later. I'm at home."

"N-no...I mean, we've been discussing what Dr. Siricca told you and me about Amy. Please don't hang up."

"I won't."

"Good. Just a moment."

She switched back to her mother. "Mom? It's Gideon."

"Then you get back to him. Phone me later."

"Okay." She cleared her throat. "Thanks for listening."

"You know I'm always here. Just make me one promise."

"What's that?"

"Bring Gideon by the house tomorrow. Your father and I want to meet him."

"I will. Good night, Mom."

"Good night, honey."

Heidi went back to Gideon's call. "Sorry to keep you waiting."

"If anyone's sorry, *I* am—for the way Fay burst in on us earlier this evening. For what it's worth, she's never done anything like that before."

"It's all right, Gideon."

"No," he countered. "What she did in using Kevin's key to gain entrance without warning us was a malicious act. It made you so uncomfortable you felt you had to leave my home.''

''Please forgive me for slipping away without letting you know.''

''You don't need to explain anything,'' he said in even tones. ''My ex-wife was out of control. But for once, there were consequences.''

Adrenaline surged through her body. ''What do you mean?''

''Kevin's going to be living with me from now on.''

''You mean she gave up custody?'' she asked, astonished by this turn of events.

''Only long enough to tear you and me apart, or so she supposes. What she doesn't realize is that it's final, as far as Kevin is concerned. He's been begging for this for a long time. Naturally I couldn't be happier.'' The joy in his voice was unmistakable.

Tears filled her eyes. ''Oh, Gideon, I know how much you and Kevin love each other. No matter how it came about, it's wonderful!''

''I have to thank you for being so understanding of what has been a delicate situation up to now,'' he said, his voice husky.

Her hand tightened on her cell phone. ''I imagine you'll have to proceed carefully with him for a while.''

''I'm going for a run with him and Pokey now. That's when I'll tell him I'm bringing you back here tonight.''

''No, don't do that!'' Her voice shook. ''This is his first night with you under these new arrangements. He needs his father to himself. It's been a long time coming.''

She heard a muffled groan. "I'd give anything not to have any distance separating us right now. Then you'd find out just how much you mean to me."

"Maybe it's better we're apart, because I feel the same way," she confessed.

"Heidi, listen. I'll run Kevin to school in the morning, then come by for you around eight-fifteen."

"I'll be ready."

"Don't unpack your suitcase. You'll need it for the rest of the week."

He said goodbye and quickly ended the call, making it impossible for her to respond.

Gideon had sounded so definite just now, but she had a hunch he'd forgotten his son's declaration about not wanting to watch his father teach the criminology course anymore. If Kevin still felt that way, he certainly wouldn't be thrilled to find out he had to share his father with her *after* class, too.

THE DOG STARTED to bark.

"Hey, Dad!" Kevin stood at the sink, filling the dishwasher after their dinner of grilled cheese-and-ham sandwiches. "Max and Gaby just drove up."

"I know." Gideon crossed to the counter to cover the bowl of leftover salad with foil. "Before I met you on the beach, I called and asked them to come over."

"You mean…"

"I thought we'd celebrate."

Kevin beamed. "Did you tell them about me?"

"Nope. That's your surprise."

"You're the greatest, Dad!" He hugged him hard, then ran to the back door to let their guests inside.

"Guess what?" he cried. "I'm living with Dad from now on!"

Max flashed Gideon a glance of surprise as he and Gaby began to make a big fuss over Kevin and Pokey.

"Ice-cream sundaes coming up," Gideon announced.

Gaby joined him by the refrigerator and they hugged. "Mmm. I shouldn't do this when I have a doctor's appointment tomorrow, but I can't say no to chocolate fudge."

Gideon grinned, then patted her swollen stomach. "Your little guy or girl will love it," he teased.

She lifted starry eyes to him. "I hope he looks just like Max."

"You know it's a boy?"

"No. It's just a feeling I have."

"What are you two whispering about?" Max asked.

"What do you think?" Gideon threw back at his friend, who chuckled.

Soon everyone was settled in the family room enjoying dessert.

Max eyed Gideon, then Kevin. "So, tell us how this miracle happened for our favorite fourteen-year-old."

"I've been begging Mom for a long time. Today she said she had something important to tell Dad and brought me over here."

"That's right," Gideon interceded. "She came straight to the point, then left without him."

Max's wife leaned forward. "Other than learning I was pregnant, I think this is the best news I've ever heard."

"Yeah. Me, too." Kevin's face was wreathed in smiles.

"I think this calls for some fun on your new Play Station, Kevin," Gaby said. "Whoever wins two out of three games has to treat the other to a movie this weekend. How about it?"

"You're on!"

She looked at Max, then Gideon. "We'll be back later, guys."

"Yeah," Kevin joined in. "Much later."

Gideon watched them leave the room. Bless her. She knew how much he needed to talk to Max alone.

"Damned if my wife's not better at those computer games than I am."

"Those, *and* stickball."

"Don't remind me," Max groaned. "I thought pregnancy might slow her down, but..."

"Well, all I can say is, you're a lucky couple."

They smiled at each other in perfect understanding. Then Max's smile faded. "What really happened with Kevin?"

"To put it bluntly, Heidi and I had just removed ourselves to the bedroom when we heard voices in the kitchen. Fay used Kevin's house key to walk in unannounced."

Max's brow furrowed. "Did she know Heidi was here?"

"She hoped."

Max muttered an oath. "Tell me what's been going on."

It was a relief to confide in his friend. They discussed Fay and Kevin at some length. Then the subject switched to Heidi. After sharing his personal feelings, Gideon filled Max in on the details of the Turner case. Finally he expounded his theory that it was a suicide meant to look like murder.

"I'm getting close, Max, but I need your help with one part of the investigation. It could be the most important part."

"What do you want me to do?"

"Something tells me Amy was on drugs at the time. The autopsy might or might not confirm it. There are two women, Kristen and Stacy, who testified at the trial on her behalf. They would know. It's possible they're drug users, too.

"Assuming that's the case, I want to know who supplied them. On the day Amy died, she tried to get a semester's worth of tuition money from her parents."

Max nodded. "She probably needed it to buy more drugs—get stoned in order to go through with the suicide."

"I agree. She wasn't successful with her parents, though. I'd like to find out if she got the money someplace else. If not, maybe she had a long-enough track record with one supplier that she could go to him in desperation and promise to pay later. He'd know she was good for the money."

"It's possible."

"Here's a photocopy of the trial transcript." Gideon lifted it from the end table and put it in Max's hands. "All the names you need are in there. At the time of the trial, Amy's friends were attending an acting college here in San Diego. I don't know what's happened to them since."

"I'll read it through tonight, then give you a call in the morning."

"You're sure it's not asking too much on top of your normal caseload?"

"Come on, Gideon. You think I don't know what it'll mean to you to get Dana released from prison? Gabriella and I can hardly wait to meet Heidi. Bring her and Kevin to dinner tomorrow before your class. While the women get acquainted, we'll plan a strategy."

"Have you talked to Gaby about this?"

"We discussed the idea in the car on the way over. Little did we know we'd find Kevin living with you on a permanent basis. That's great news. I couldn't be happier for you."

Gideon nodded. "Of course, you know Fay. In a few days she's going to scream foul."

"Her jealousy of Heidi has cost her more than she bargained for this time," Max said fiercely. "No matter how she tries to manipulate Kevin now, it won't get her anywhere."

Fay had alienated Max as far back as New York. He had little patience with her.

"I could have pushed it two years ago, but I'm glad I didn't. It's much better this way. He's older now, and he knows the truth about everything. That makes him less vulnerable than before."

"I agree." Max sat forward. "How does Kevin feel about Heidi?"

Gideon was silent for a moment. Then, "For starters, he made a scene in front of Heidi and me at a Mexican restaurant.'' Gideon told him the details that had led to the hospital incident. "Kevin hasn't shown any overt hostility toward her tonight, but we have to remember his mother stole the spotlight. I'll find out the true state of affairs when Heidi and I pick him up at school tomorrow.''

"Well, it's late.'' Getting to his feet, Max said, "We need to leave so you two can go to bed. I'm ready to call it a night myself. My pregnant wife has trouble sleeping and will want to discuss every detail of this case with me.''

Gideon grimaced as he eyed the photocopy. "Dana's case can't get solved soon enough for me. I feel like I'm standing on the brink of something marvelous with Heidi, but...''

"But you can't jump in with both feet yet,'' Max said. "I went through the same thing last August with Gabriella. It was heaven and hell.''

"You're right about that.''

Max clasped his shoulder. "I'll do everything I can to help. If the autopsy reveals evidence of drugs, we'll get a search warrant so we can check out the places Amy's girlfriends live.''

"Sounds like a plan. Thanks for coming over. You guys made this into a terrific night for Kevin. It's what we both needed.''

"Take it from me, what *you* need is the right wife.''

Gideon's eyes closed. "I figured that out the night I met Heidi.''

"It's going to happen.''

"It has to, Max.''

HEIDI AWOKE EARLY Wednesday morning so excited to see Gideon she was ready long before he'd said he'd come by.

She would've loved to pretend she was running late. Then she'd invite him in. The moment they shut the door, they'd pick up where they left off last night. She knew what would happen if he touched her....

Even when Gideon wasn't around, she ached for him. Just thinking about him made her body tremble with desire. But she had to resist her feelings for Gideon—because of his son.

Until Kevin could like her for herself, he wouldn't be able to accept her in his father's life. That could take a long time. She refused to think *never,* but this was a teenager with some serious insecurities.

Now Kevin would be living with Gideon. He'd probably dreamed about having his dad around all day, every day, an arrangement most of his other friends took for granted.

Heidi's mere presence could fracture the beautiful picture Kevin no doubt carried in his mind—father, son and dog facing the world together.

She put herself in Kevin's place, recognizing that the last thing she'd want was some strange woman taking up space in his dad's house, vying for his dad's attention.

He finally had a chance to be with his father, to live the life he wanted. Heidi couldn't wreck that for Kevin. She wouldn't!

Gideon had told her not to unpack her bag. It stood by the front door waiting for his return.

"No! It's not going to happen!" she cried to the empty apartment. Marching across the room, she picked the bag up and took it to the bedroom, where she put everything away.

How could she even think about her wants and needs when Kevin was so fragile and Dana still languished in prison?

Shocked by her own selfishness, Heidi acknowledged how complicated everything had become since she'd joined Gideon's class. Deep in thought, she jumped when she heard the knock at her door.

"Heidi?" Gideon called out.

He was early!

She'd planned to run out to the car as soon as she saw it pull up at the curb. Now it was too late. Her heartbeat accelerated to a violent tattoo.

Halfway to the door, she halted. "Gideon, I'm not quite ready." *I have to think what I'm going to do about you.* "Could you just wait for me in the car? I'll be down as soon as I can."

"Open the door, Heidi."

His request sounded more like a command, and she started to shake.

"Heidi!"

She gave in and darted to the door, then swung it open. Like lightning, Gideon backed her into the apartment and covered her mouth with his. A voracious hunger seemed to be driving him.

He finally tore his lips from hers. "Do you have any idea how I felt when I walked into the kitchen last night and discovered you'd gone?"

"You *know* why I left," she murmured as his mouth roamed her face with restless intensity, kissing her eyes, her nose, her cheeks and throat. Freshly shaved, he smelled of the soap he used in the shower. It worked like an aphrodisiac on her.

He plunged his hands in her hair, raising her head up so their eyes could meet. "Don't ever do that to me again. My heart won't take it another time."

"Neither will mine. That's why I can't stay at your house."

He frowned. "You already have, so that argument won't wash."

"Kevin hadn't moved in then, Gideon."

"He has his own bedroom."

"That's not the point and you know it!" Her voice trembled. "We have to give him time. If I were Kevin, I wouldn't want some woman around, either."

"You're not just some woman!"

"Listen to me, Gideon. You're his father. He adores you. This is the first time he's been able to live with you since the divorce. Think what it means to him."

Gideon shook his head. "I have needs, too, Heidi. I want you there with me tonight, tomorrow and all the days and nights after that."

She couldn't get through to him. He'd begun kissing her again. Deep, searching kisses that drew the response she seemed incapable of withholding from him. Somehow she had to stop this before they reached the point of no return.

Pushing against his chest, she managed to wrench herself from his arms and take several steps back.

"No." She raised her hands when he would have touched her again. "Don't come any closer, Gideon."

Her comment checked his movements. "Is there

something you're not telling me?'' he asked. A shadow crossed his face.

His ex-wife's betrayal had left scars.

''There's no one else, and you know it!'' she rushed to reassure him. ''I want to be with you every second, too! But until Kevin welcomes me into that circle he's drawn around the two of you, we *can't* take whatever we want. Otherwise we'll jeopardize the little we already have.''

His chest heaved with the strength of his emotions. ''So what are you suggesting?''

''That we go on as we have been, without my staying at your house. By the time we can get Dana's case reopened, maybe Kevin won't feel so threatened.

''I remember an old saying—first we hate, then we tolerate and finally embrace. I don't think Kevin hates me. But your house is *his* house now. Can't you see that if I stay in the bedroom next to his, it'll be like shoving something distasteful down his throat? He's not ready for me to be part of your life yet, Gideon.''

When Gideon didn't answer, she made another attempt to reason with him. ''If we can get him used to my presence, then we'll have made a lot of progress.''

His eyes narrowed. ''Children by definition are selfish creatures. If we follow your scenario, Kevin could hold us hostage indefinitely.''

Heidi rubbed her forehead, where she could feel the beginnings of a headache. ''We still have to consider his feelings. At least for a while,'' she added quietly.

After a long pause, he muttered, ''I'm willing to go along with that for a short period, provided you won't allow him to manipulate our relationship in other ways.''

''I...I don't understand.''

''I think you do,'' he said smoothly. ''When we pick him up after school today and he says he doesn't plan to come to the class with us, I don't want you bowing out with some made-up excuse in order to spare his feelings.''

She wondered how to stand her ground and still placate Gideon. ''Why don't we agree to deal with one situation at a time?''

He sighed. ''Tonight we have two situations,'' he told her. ''Max and Gaby have invited the three of us to dinner before class. They want to meet you.''

She lifted her head, rearranging the swirl of red-gold hair around her shoulders. ''I'd love to get to know them.''

His jaw hardened. ''Even if Kevin chooses not to go with us?''

For some reason, Heidi sensed that were she to say the wrong thing now, it could hurt Gideon. She didn't know why, but for the first time she wondered if he wasn't as fragile as Kevin in his own way.

''Whatever he decides to do—stay at your place or accompany us—I plan to be with you until you bring me back home tonight.''

Strong arms shot out to pull her against him. ''Be very certain that's what you want.''

Or what?

Will I lose you?

That possibility was so terrifying, she sought blindly for his mouth, eager to prove he was her whole world.

At first his kiss was almost savage in its possession, as if he was testing her need of him. When it got through to him that she was the one who clung with primitive longing, she heard a satisfied groan before his body finally relaxed, allowing her to breathe again.

Whatever had been troubling him seemed to have vanished.

CHAPTER THIRTEEN

WHEN SHE SAW the name Jim Varney on the sign in front of the bank teller's window, Heidi darted Gideon a meaningful glance. Since their visit to the gas station yesterday, she'd made several phone calls to locate the former garage attendant's whereabouts.

After the person ahead of them had finished her transaction, Heidi stepped up to the window.

The sandy-haired man behind the counter studied her with blatant masculine interest. "May I help you, ma'am?" He had a pronounced Southern accent.

"I hope so. My name is Heidi Ellis. Didn't you used to work at Lyle's Gas Station in Mission Bay? My family still goes there."

"Yes, ma'am. I worked there for a short time last spring." His face broke into a fulsome smile. "I don't recall seeing you—I know I would've remembered."

"I guess I went in for gas when you were off duty." She turned to Gideon. "Allow me to introduce Detective Poletti. He's from the San Diego Homicide division."

The other man's smile faded. "Hello, sir."

Gideon nodded. "Good morning, Mr. Varney. I'm investigating a murder case." He flashed his ID. "Do you think you could ask someone to cover for you so we could talk privately? It will only take a moment.''

The younger man looked taken back. "Uh, sure. Why don't you sit down by the desk over in the loans department? I'll be right there.''

"I think he's frightened to death,'' Heidi whispered as they moved to the other side of the small branch office and sat down.

"My badge only has that effect on people with something to hide. If he stopped smiling, it's because you introduced us before he had a chance to make a move on you.''

"You're wrong about that!''

"Like hell I am,'' he countered without a trace of amusement. "The guy could hardly function for checking you out.''

"That's absurd.''

"He's not the only male who's interested. If you doubt me, take a look at the three men in line. They can't take their eyes off you.''

"Gideon, come on.'' She didn't know him in this mood. Without conscious thought she reached for his hand. "I didn't realize you could be so grumpy,'' she teased in an effort to coax a smile out of him.

"Sometimes in the morning,'' he conceded after a brief silence. It was the first show of levity since he'd picked her up at her apartment. His eyes continued to probe hers. "You don't have a vain bone in your body, do you.''

Heat crept into her face.

Jim Varney chose that moment to join them. He sat

down at the desk. Gideon was still holding her hand, a fact the other man couldn't help but notice.

"I'm free now," he said. "What did you want to talk to me about?"

With a final squeeze Gideon let go of her hand, then pulled the gas receipt from his pocket and placed it on the desk.

"Are those your initials, Mr. Varney?"

The other man studied the slip. "Yes, sir."

"As you can see, Dana Turner was the woman who signed for the gas. Does that name mean anything to you?"

"No, sir," he said without hesitation.

"You mean you don't remember the Turner murder? It happened in Mission Bay?"

"Oh, yeah—I heard something about it later in the year, but I'd just taken my finals at the university and I flew home to Houston for the summer. Now I'm back here in graduate school."

This man's testimony was pivotal to Dana's case. Heidi could barely sit still.

"If I showed you some pictures, do you think you could identify the woman who came in? According to this slip, she bought two gallons of gas from you."

The teller hunched his shoulders. "I don't know. That was almost a year ago. I can try."

"Good."

Gideon reached in his pocket and placed a half-dozen colored photographs of various brunettes, including the one of Dana, on the desk. Heidi decided he must've made an early run to police headquarters this morning to get the other pictures. All were face and shoulder shots.

"Take your time, Mr. Varney."

As the man picked up one picture after another, Heidi held her breath. It didn't take him long to make a decision. He shook his head. "None of these women look familiar."

"You're sure?"

Once again, he studied the photos. "I'm positive I've never waited on any of these ladies."

He hadn't recognized Dana.

Gideon scooped them up, then put down two more. "How about these redheads?"

"No," came the emphatic answer. His eyes swerved to Heidi. "You don't forget hair that color."

If Gideon noticed the other man's personal glance, he didn't let it show. Instead, he removed the pictures and put down four more, which included Amy's. All the women were blondes.

"I don't know," the man murmured. He studied the photographs for another minute before tapping Amy's. Gideon's professional demeanor was firmly in place; he revealed no reaction whatsoever. But Heidi was so excited by what Jim Varney was telling them, her heart was pounding erratically and her palms were damp.

"She looks kind of familiar, but with just a face it's hard to be sure. I *might* have waited on her."

"Will this help?"

Gideon pulled out a wallet-size snap of Amy with her two actress friends. He handed it to the other man. Heidi supposed he'd gotten it from the police archives.

The second Varney saw it, he started to nod. "That's

her. Short and blond. After I filled up her gas can and put it in the back of her Jeep, I remember thinking she'd have trouble if she tried to carry it herself.''

Heidi sat there, overwhelmed with gratitude to this young man. Everything added up. *Amy drove a Jeep.* Through the roaring in her ears, she heard Gideon ask, ''You can still recall the make of car?''

''In this case I do. A Jeep doesn't have a trunk. Her hardtop was still on, and gas fumes can get pretty bad. I said I hoped she didn't have far to drive. She made a face at me and told me not to worry about it. I guess she thought I was patronizing her.''

That sounded like Amy.

Heidi grabbed hold of Gideon's forearm. ''Amy drove a hardtop Wrangler,'' she whispered to him.

He nodded. ''Mr. Varney? Are you certain enough about what you've just told us to be willing to testify to it in a court of law?''

''Yes, sir.''

''Then you'll be hearing from a Mr. John Cobb within a week. He's a criminal lawyer here in San Diego, and he'll want to talk to you. Thanks for your cooperation.''

If she'd been alone and felt the bank teller wouldn't take it the wrong way, Heidi would've hugged him. As it was, she had to follow Gideon's lead, maintaining her composure for as long as it took to reach his car.

But once they were inside, she let go with an ecstatic cry. Despite the console separating their seats, she flung her arms around his neck. ''You did it! You got it out of him! You're amazing and brilliant and fantastic! His testimony *proves* Dana didn't go near the filling station that day.''

Too choked up to say another word, all she could do was cling to him.

He drew her closer, burying his face in her hair. ''I need to phone John Cobb with this news. Varney's testimony, plus Dr. Siricca's medical opinion that Amy was disturbed, now allows us to color in all the fours and fives of our painting. We're halfway there. By the weekend it should be finished.''

She lifted her head to look into his eyes. ''What will happen then?''

''Cobb will prepare a motion for a notice of hearing before the judge who had jurisdiction over Dana's case. The same notice will be delivered to Jenke.

''As soon as he receives it, the phone lines are going to burn between his office and Cobb's. In the meantime the judge will set a court date for the evidentiary hearing.''

''Will there be a jury?''

''Not if the evidence is so convincing that the judge vacates his original verdict. However, if he decides there's still reasonable doubt, he'll order another trial with a new jury. But I'd hate to see Dana put through that experience again.''

Heidi shivered. ''So would I.''

''That's why we're going to fill in every number of our painting first.''

On that note he kissed her long and hard. When he eventually released her, she blushed; a number of people in the bank parking lot were watching them.

A seductive smile lingered on his lips, the first smile

Heidi had seen all morning. Relieved his mood seemed lighter now, she sat back in her seat.

"You were naughty to do that in front of an audience."

"Are you talking about what we were *both* doing—with equal enthusiasm, I might add? I have news for you, sweetheart." At the endearment, she felt her heart turn over. "That wasn't naughty. You'll recognize naughty when it happens," he murmured, starting the car and pulling onto the road. "Trust me."

Unable to resist, she said, "Is that a promise?"

"You shouldn't ask me a question like that in heavy traffic."

She fought a smile. "Where are we going now?"

"To the Turners again," he told her. "Ed called me early this morning. He and Christine went to the phone company yesterday and got copies of all the phone bills I requested. The four of us should be able to figure out any calls that can't be accounted for."

"You think she'd dare use her parents' phone to get in touch with a drug dealer?"

While they were stopped at a traffic light, Gideon turned to her. "Maybe. Don't forget, she was planning her own death, but wanted Dana punished for it."

"So what you're saying is, she wouldn't have left a trail from her own cell phone for the police to investigate."

"She had total access to her parents' empty house five days of every week. With them working full-time and Dana living in Pasadena—"

"You're right!"

"There's something else, Heidi."

She could hardly keep up with him. "What?"

"Ed and Christine are very trusting, very laid-back. Their daughters' being able to charge gas whenever they needed to, no questions asked, is just an example of that."

Heidi nodded. "They're generous to a fault."

"Dana's parents don't strike me as the kind of people to pore over the phone bill every month working out who owes what. Amy knew their lives were too full of important matters to worry about details. She probably took full advantage of that."

"I don't doubt it for a second."

"Do you know if they're on the Internet?"

When his question sank in, Heidi said, "Her e-mail! Of course!"

"That, too, but I was thinking more of chat rooms and Web sites she might have visited. They would reveal how much time she actually spent on-line—and what she was up to."

Heidi's thoughts leaped ahead. "Shouldn't the Turners' credit card bills be checked, too?"

He gave her leg a gentle squeeze. "You're reading my mind again."

"Gideon, Amy was obviously so sick it wouldn't surprise me if she had her own Web site and charged the setup fee to her parents."

"None of this is outside the realm of possibility."

"Before Christmas we had an incident at school. A kid who was a library aide got hold of his dad's credit card. Without anyone's knowledge he and his friends had a hate Web site constructed. They ran it from the computer lab in the library until another student found out. Not only the police but the FBI were called in.''

''It happens far too often.'' He sighed. ''But Internet crime isn't a problem we can solve today.'' He smiled slightly. ''We have enough to do before we run by Kevin's school at three.''

At the mention of his son, she looked down at her hands.

''He knows you'll be with me, Heidi.''

''What if he's not there waiting?''

''Then it means he needs to go in for some serious counseling.''

She took a shaky breath. ''I'm afraid.''

''Kevin's learned the art of manipulation from a master teacher.''

He was referring to his ex-wife of course. The bitterness in his voice was the residue of pain he'd suffered at her hands.

Heidi sensed that Gideon needed her to assure him she wouldn't be intimidated. But she didn't honestly know how long she could bear to be the one distancing Kevin from his father.

''Tell me what you're thinking.''

Unable to say the words, she felt a new tension spring between them. It continued to build while they were at the Turners'. Except for one phone number that no one recognized, they found nothing to help them as they looked through the few undeleted e-mail messages.

By the time Gideon pulled up in front of Oakdale Middle School at three, his emotional withdrawal was complete. It hurt her so badly, she didn't even realize

Kevin had run up to the car until she heard the back door open.

"Hi, Dad!"

"Hi, yourself."

When he got in and shut it again, she turned to look at him. "How are you, Kevin?"

"Fine." He suddenly leaned forward to whisper something to Gideon.

She cringed when his father said, "If you have something to tell me, you can say it in front of Heidi."

Though Gideon hadn't spoken unkindly, Kevin obviously took it as an admonishment. He sat back without another word.

Silence reigned the whole distance to the Calders' beachfront home in La Jolla. The second Gideon pulled into their driveway, Kevin got out of the car and disappeared through an archway connecting the Spanish-style house to the garage.

As Gideon came around to open the door for Heidi, the bleak look in his eyes was so disturbing she wanted to take him in her arms. But she couldn't do that because their hostess had chosen that moment to appear.

The stunning—and very pregnant—brunette hugged Gideon, then turned to Heidi. "I've heard a lot about you. All of it terrific. I'm Gaby Calder." The warmth in her smile was heartfelt. Welcoming.

"I've heard wonderful things about you, too. I'm Heidi Ellis."

The two of them shook hands before Gaby took her arm. "Come on out to the veranda. Max is fixing drinks for you. White wine okay? Until our baby's born, I'm reduced to drinking soda, along with Kevin,'' she confided.

"You're so lucky to be having a baby,'' Heidi whispered.

"Believe me, I know it,'' Gaby whispered back.

A moment later Heidi was introduced to Max. Like Gideon, he was a tall, dark, powerfully built man. He smiled at her; despite his apparent approval, she sensed that he was watching her carefully.

"Where's Kevin?'' he asked.

Gaby glanced toward the ocean. "I told him about some starfish that were swept in by the tide early this morning. He ran down to look at them.''

Heidi bit her lip. "Did he seem okay to you?''

The other woman eyed her with compassion as she handed her a glass of wine. "Come into the kitchen while I finish getting dinner ready.''

Thankful for a sensitive person who understood Gideon's son, she followed Gaby into the house.

"Oh—how beautiful!'' The gleaming white of the kitchen was offset by dark wood beams and exquisite tile work in deep reds, blues, greens and yellows.

Gaby smiled. "I'm crazy about it, too!''

"How could you not be? I'd kill for a kitchen like this! So would my mother!'' Heidi then proceeded to tell Gaby about some of the furniture imported by their family business.

"I'm going to have to visit her store. Except for the nursery, the rest of the house has a long way to go before it's furnished the way we want. After dinner I'll show it to you.'' She placed the steaks on the hot grill.

"Can I do anything to help?'' Heidi asked.

"No, everything's under control." Gaby raised her eyebrows. "Do you have any idea how many women around here have been in pursuit of San Diego's most elusive bachelor?"

Heidi's face went hot.

"You *should* blush," Gaby remarked. "According to my husband, there are *lots*."

"Kevin's the reason he stayed single. Now that his mother's said he can live with Gideon, he deserves to come first in his father's life."

"If you've been telling Gideon that, then it's no wonder he looked so furious when he arrived." She turned the steaks. "Do you love him?"

"Yes!" Heidi said in a tremulous whisper.

"Have you told him?"

"N-not in so many words. We haven't known each other that long."

"Max and I fell in love at first sight."

"That's what Gideon told me. But in our situation there's still so much at stake."

Gaby stared her down. "He needs the words, Heidi. He needs the love of a woman like you who'll fight for him."

"Even if it hurts Kevin?"

"Kevin's always had the love of both his parents. He's never known betrayal. The person who needs healing is Gideon." After a pause she asked, "What are you afraid of?"

"That I'll be the reason Kevin goes back to his mother's. It would break Gideon's heart."

"No. You're the only person who can do that,"

Gaby countered. "I hope you realize it before it's too late."

GIDEON PUSHED AWAY from the table. "As usual the meal was superb, Gaby, but I'm afraid the three of us have to go or we won't make it to class on time."

"The steak was delicious," Heidi concurred, "but I have to say the linguini and clams were absolutely incredible."

"I second that." Max gave his wife a resounding kiss.

"Your chocolate-mint pie was great!" Kevin said enthusiastically.

Gaby smiled at him. "I made it just for you. Come on. I'll walk you and Heidi to the car."

Gideon watched them leave the kitchen, then turned to Max. "Your wife outdid herself. That dinner was one of the best I've had in months. No, years."

"We've been anxious to meet the woman you've fallen for—and fallen hard, I might say. So we wanted this evening to be special." He paused. "Heidi Ellis is a knockout, in more ways than one."

"Believe me, I know."

"You want to hear my advice?" Their eyes met. "Like me, you had to wait all these years for the right woman to come along. Now that you've found her, don't waste another second."

"I don't intend to," Gideon said. "That's why I want to finish up this investigation by the weekend."

"After reading that court case last night, Gabriella had nightmares."

"I'm not surprised."

"Did you find anything interesting on the Turners' computer?"

"No. But there's a phone number that needs to be checked out."

"Give it to me and I'll do it."

"I'd appreciate that. How are thing at your end?"

"This morning I contacted Officer Crandall. He's in Balboa Park running surveillance on Kristen and Stacy's apartment. I'll be joining him in another half hour. We'll interview the neighbors to see what we can learn. Then we'll ask the girls some questions. Expect a call from me around midnight."

Gideon nodded. "Sounds good. I owe you."

"I'll consider all debts paid in full when you tell me you're leaving Kevin here for a couple of weeks because you're going on your honeymoon."

"Lord, don't I wish."

"The woman's crazy about you."

"Maybe."

"What do you mean?"

"Heidi's afraid Kevin won't accept her. She's terrified of hurting him."

"I like her better and better."

"So do I. Thanks for everything. I've got to run."

Gideon hurried out to the car. Just as he'd feared, Kevin sat in the back chatting with Gaby through the window while Heidi was ignored.

He gave Max's wife a hug, then slid behind the wheel and turned on the ignition. "What do you think of the Calders?" he asked once they'd merged with the traffic.

"They're lovely people. I can't believe what a fabulous cook she is."

"Kevin and I won't argue with that."

When he couldn't get a response out of his son, he decided to concentrate on the woman seated next to him. He could feel her fear of saying or doing the wrong thing around Kevin. Damn, the situation infuriated him!

Max's words rang in his ears. *Now that you've found her, don't waste another second.*

Craving contact, he reached for her hand and threaded his fingers through hers. He could feel the tiny pulse beats. She tried to pull away, which only increased his determination to hold on. After a few seconds she gave up the struggle.

He began stroking her palm with his thumb. Her body quickened at his touch. He was satisfied to feel that much response, his frustration mollified, at least for the moment.

DESPITE HIS EARLIER declaration, Kevin entered the school with them, but his continued silence, apparently aimed at his father, made the situation unbearable for Heidi. The presence of the animated writers standing outside her classroom had never been more welcome.

Once Gideon had unlocked the door, Heidi rushed inside to set up the chairs. It was a relief to have something to do with her nervous energy. As she looked carefully around the room, pleased that the substitutes were keeping everything in order, she saw Kevin take his usual place and open his backpack.

No sooner had she sat in her chair at one end of the

semicircle than their guest speaker appeared at the door. The fiftyish-looking man with dark hair and a wiry build greeted Gideon as though they were old friends.

Heidi paid particular attention to him because he was the person who would be doing the autopsy on Amy's body in the morning.

Gideon stood next to him. "Good evening, everyone. As promised, our guest speaker is renowned for the impeccable work he does as coroner here in San Diego.

"He's the best of the best. We're extremely fortunate he agreed to take time out of his busy schedule to present tonight's lecture. Please give a hearty welcome to Dr. Carlos Diaz."

Heidi clapped, along with everyone else. She cast a glance at Kevin to see his reaction. The teen kept his head averted.

The other man cleared his throat. "I'm honored that Detective Poletti has asked me to address this august group of mystery writers. He sang your praises. What could I do except say yes?" He smiled.

"You may not know this, but he's a legend in the San Diego Police Department. That makes me doubly honored to be here.

"I'll let you in on a little secret about myself. I used to write science-fiction stories when I was the age of Gideon's son back there. I have no idea how good they were because I wouldn't show them to anybody."

A ripple of comments about understanding exactly how he'd felt ran through the group.

"It takes courage to put what comes out of your

heart, your brain and soul, on paper. I commend you for your efforts. If anything I say tonight can help make your work more authentic and professional, then I'll feel compensated.''

For the rest of the evening, he completely held their interest—a truly captive audience. Heidi was so fascinated by his presentation she protested like the others when the bell rang signaling the end of class.

They all rushed forward to congregate around him and Gideon. As Heidi started to straighten chairs, she noticed Kevin slip out the door.

She would've run after him, but she knew he'd reject any attempt of hers to be friendly. The situation was getting worse by the minute. Surely Gideon would agree that if Kevin continued to be difficult, they would have to rethink their relationship.

Suddenly he was beside her. His arm went around her waist. ''Carlos, this is Heidi Ellis, the woman I told you about.''

''How do you do, Dr. Diaz. Your talk held us absolutely spellbound.''

The man's dark eyes flashed with pleasure as he shook her hand. ''So you're the one fighting for your friend's freedom. Tomorrow I'll do my best to be as thorough as possible.''

Her eyes brimmed with tears. ''Words are inadequate, but they're all I have to let you know my gratitude. Thank you, Dr. Diaz.''

''You're welcome.'' His gaze swerved to Gideon's. ''I'm going to start early. Call me around ten in the morning and I should be able to tell you what I found. Let's hope it helps.''

Gideon shook his hand. "We appreciate your getting it done this fast."

The second the door shut behind Dr. Diaz, Gideon turned her in his arms. His blue gaze burned into hers.

"Finally I've got you alone for a minute."

She knew he wanted to kiss her, but she couldn't forget that his son was waiting for them—maybe just outside the door.

"No, Gideon!" she cried, evading his mouth. "We can't do this while Kevin's with us. When we get to my apartment, please let me go in by myself. We can talk tomorrow after you drop him off at school."

Twisting out of reach, she hurried into the hall, half expecting to find Kevin. Relieved he wasn't there, she continued walking.

Gideon caught up to her near the office. His expression was so forbidding she practically ran out the doors to the car.

Kevin was leaning against the trunk of the Acura. He straightened when he saw them coming. Afraid to look him in the face, she lowered her eyes while Gideon opened her door.

"What did you think about what you heard tonight, Kevin?" he asked when he'd climbed into the driver's seat.

"I didn't hear that much because I was doing my math."

"That's too bad. It was an opportunity to learn about a subject few people understand. Dr. Diaz's expertise might be the deciding factor in getting Dana Turner out of prison."

Heidi waited for a response from Kevin. When it

became clear that nothing was forthcoming, she stirred restlessly in her seat. If she could be thankful for one thing, it was that she lived close to the school. The drive home, with its agonizing silence, was about to come to an end.

After what she'd said to Gideon in the classroom, she assumed he'd pull away from the curb once she got out of the car. To her shock, he turned off the ignition and came around to her side.

"Good night, Kevin," she called to his son.

"Good night," he answered in a flat voice.

When she unlocked her apartment door seconds later, Gideon followed her inside and shut it. She'd left a lamp on. In the soft light the pained grimace of his features filled her with fresh dismay.

"We're going to have that talk tomorrow," he said in a gravelly tone. "Until then, this will have to do."

His mouth descended with a hunger that reached deep inside her. As he enfolded her in his arms, she sensed, for the first time, what Gaby had been trying to tell her earlier. Inside this strong heroic man lived a soul that was yearning to be whole again.

In that instant she determined she was going to win Kevin around, because Gideon was life to her. She would fight for him, no matter what.

CHAPTER FOURTEEN

IT WAS ONE IN THE MORNING; Max should have phoned by now. Gideon threw off the covers and got to his feet. After the strained evening Kevin had caused him and Heidi, sleep was out of the question.

But Gideon couldn't blame his son for all his restlessness. Something else was haunting him. When he looked back on his relationship with Heidi, he realized *he'd* been the one to make every physical overture. Never once since they'd met had she taken the initiative.

She'd always responded to his kisses of course. Tonight at the apartment was a case in point. But was it only because he'd forced it?

Not for the first time, he asked himself if he was too old for her. Max had assured him otherwise, but after today more doubts had crept in. Was he fooling himself by believing she cared as much as he did?

Maybe the situation with Kevin was too difficult for a twenty-six-year-old woman who'd never been married.

Fay's barb about Heidi being so young had found its mark, after all.

Unable to tolerate the blackness of his own thoughts, he dressed in his sweats and tiptoed out of his bedroom to the kitchen. In case Kevin awoke, he left a note on the counter. It said he was taking a short run on the beach and would be back by one-thirty.

He put his cell phone in the pocket of his hooded top and slipped out the back door without a coat. The fog had rolled in thick and misty.

He broke into a run, needing the workout to rid himself of built-up tension. Heidi's presence in his life had brought on dreams he'd never dreamed, not even after meeting Fay. He hadn't been mature enough back then to understand the richness life could hold, or the emptiness when it wasn't right.

With Heidi he could see himself having everything he'd thought was beyond his reach. But that wouldn't happen—*couldn't* happen—if she wasn't dreaming the same dreams. This fear was what tormented him now.

The kitchen light was on when he returned to the house. No doubt Pokey had heard him leave and had disturbed Kevin.

Before he put his key in the lock, his son opened the door. He stared at Gideon without saying anything.

"I'm sorry if I worried you by leaving the house, Kev." He locked the door behind him.

"You didn't."

"I'm glad. Let's go back to bed, shall we?"

He turned off the light and started for his room. Kevin followed with Pokey.

Gideon took off his sweats and headed for the shower. When he came out in his robe, Kevin was sitting on the bed waiting for him.

"Dad? Can I talk to you for a minute?"

"I've had a long day. Can it wait until tomorrow?"

"I don't think so."

Gideon took a steadying breath. "If this is about wishing I'd never met Heidi, I already know how you feel. So does she."

Kevin looked guiltily away. "This is about Mom."

"Go on." Gideon sank onto the bed next to him.

"She called me while I was in class today. When I went to the office to talk to her on the phone, she said she wanted me to come home on the bus after school. She said she'd get off work early so we could go for dinner.

"I told her we were going to Max and Gaby's. That made her cry. She said she was coming over here to talk to you because she made a big mistake about letting me live with you if you're going to marry some child bride."

Lord.

"I tried to tell you about it in the car after school, but you told me I should talk to you in front of Heidi. The thing is, I didn't want her to know what Mom said. That's private stuff, and it could hurt Heidi's feelings. I wasn't trying to be rude to her, honest. I was trying to warn you in case you brought Heidi back here. I was afraid Mom would come over and embarrass her again."

"Oh, Kevin." He threw an arm around his son. "Forgive me. I'm sorry I misunderstood."

"Then you're not going to make me go back and live with Mom?"

"No. Whatever gave you that idea?"

"Because I haven't been very nice to Heidi. I remember what you told me about Frank being scared of me. I think maybe Heidi's scared of me, too.''

If the situation wasn't so precarious, Gideon would have laughed for the sheer joy of realizing his son was finally growing up.

''I think maybe she is a little.''

''I watched you looking at her at dinner. It's the same way Max looks at Gaby. Like...like you're really happy.''

Gideon smiled. ''That's because I had my two favorite people with me. My son and the woman I want to marry.''

Kevin cocked his head. ''Have you asked her yet?''

''No. I haven't even told her I love her.''

''How come?''

''For one thing the time's not right. I'm still working to get her friend out of prison. For another she hasn't told me she loves me. Maybe she doesn't feel the same about me as I feel about her. You can't force another person to love you. It has to happen on its own.''

''She loves you, Dad.''

''I'm not so sure.''

''I am. That night in her classroom when you told her you were divorced, she got this excited look on her face. It made me mad,'' he admitted quietly. ''And then at the restaurant, before you knew I was there, Brad elbowed me and said, 'Wow—that redheaded babe sure has the hots for your dad!'''

Gideon shook his head, chuckling silently. ''I had no idea.'' In fact, he couldn't believe they were having this conversation. But he was glad of it. The darkness in his soul was starting to dissipate.

"Dad? From now on I promise to be nice to Heidi."

Gideon's heart swelled, and he gave Kevin another hug. "I can't ask for more than that."

"What if Mom comes over tomorrow?"

"It's okay if she does."

"Even if Heidi's here?"

Gideon liked the sound of that. Acceptance had been slow in coming, but they were getting there.

"Of course. In time your mother will be reconciled to the situation."

"Yeah." Kevin got up from the bed. "Mom doesn't have any room to talk. You had to get used to Frank!"

Well, well, well.

"Good night, Dad. See you in the morning. Come on, Pokey." As he left the room, he turned out the light.

Gideon slid under the covers in a much better frame of mind. If it wasn't so late, he'd call Heidi to tell her what had happened.

He wished she was here right now. In his bed. In his arms. He ached for her....

Ten minutes went by.

Max still hadn't checked in with him, which meant something must be going on. Gideon would have to wait until morning for answers.

Letting out a deep sigh, he turned over on his stomach, willing sleep to come.

When his phone finally rang, he checked his watch, incredulous to discover that he'd slept through the night and it was already seven in the morning.

Gideon reached for the phone, figuring it was Max. "Poletti here."

"Hello, Gideon?"

He'd know Heidi's voice anywhere.

Her calling this early could only mean there was a problem. He jackknifed into a sitting position, afraid she'd found some excuse not to be with him today.

"What's wrong, Heidi?"

"I guess the life of a detective automatically makes you suspicious of every phone call," she teased.

Relief coursed through him. "Guilty as charged."

"I wanted to get hold of you before you left the house. My parents would like to meet you. After you drop Kevin off at school, could you drive over to their house? You're invited for breakfast."

His eyes closed tightly. He'd been waiting for the opportunity to get to know them. Hoping…

"I'm leaving my apartment now to help Mom get things ready. She's invited the Turners, too. When I told her you'd be getting the results of the autopsy this morning, she thought we should all be together to support them, no matter what Dr. Diaz finds."

Gideon heard the tremor in her voice. A lot hinged on the autopsy; no one understood that better than Heidi.

"I'll be there by quarter to nine. Thank your mother for me."

"I already have. See you in a little while." The line went dead.

He hung up, needing to do something about the explosion of excitement he suddenly felt.

"Kevin?" He leaped out of bed and dashed down the hall to his son's room. Pokey met him at the door, jumping and barking at the commotion he'd made.

"Time to get up and shower! Rise and shine!"

"Good grief, Dad! What's gotten into you?"

"I'll tell you about it on the way to school. Come on, Pokey. Let's get you some breakfast. Too bad it's going to be nothing like mine."

Those turned out to be prophetic words.

Marjorie Ellis had prepared brunch with everything from succulent ham and eggs Benedict to scones, chocolate waffles and juicy, sweet pineapple.

Heidi kept plying him with more helpings until he could hardly move. Indeed, he had no desire to move once he'd pulled her next to him on the couch. Everyone had settled in the Ellises' living room to enjoy coffee. He never tired of the view of the bay.

In style and décor their home seemed a larger version of Heidi's apartment. He couldn't get over how much mother and daughter looked alike. Mrs. Ellis was still a lovely woman; she wore her red hair cut short in a style that suited her features.

Rowland Ellis stood as tall as Gideon. He had a dignified appearance, with patrician features and iron-gray hair. Between the two of them, he could see where Heidi got her beauty and her charm.

Gideon found that he liked her parents a great deal. They'd done everything possible to make him feel at home. As for the Turners, he'd already met them and felt a bond.

Heidi nestled comfortably against him. This would have been a perfect moment—except that Dana's life still hung in the balance.

Heidi drew back the cuffs of his shirt and suit jacket to see his watch. "It's five after ten," she whispered.

He knew what time it was.

Beads of perspiration broke out on his brow. If he was wrong about what Carlos would find...

HEIDI WATCHED HIM enter the other room to make the call, and she hugged her arms about her waist. To her surprise Dana's father got up from the chair and came to sit by her. He put a comforting arm around her shoulders.

"If it weren't for you, little Rose Red, we wouldn't be this far along. But even if, with all Gideon's help, there's to be no miracle, Christine and I want you to know what a shining light you've been in our lives.

"Dana calls you her guardian angel," he said in a tearful voice. "God has been working through you, my dear. That's something we'll never forget."

Heidi turned her head into his chest, and they wept together in the silence.

She didn't move until she noticed that her father had risen to his feet. Then she lifted her head.

Her heart jolted as she saw Gideon standing by the piano. He was very still.

"What did you find out?"

After studying her for a moment, he let his gaze settle on Dana's mother. He walked over to her and sat down.

"Christine." He covered one of her hands. "It should give you comfort to know that there was a reason your daughter couldn't help for the drastic change in her behavior. Carlos found a brain tumor the size of an orange."

Heidi's gasp joined everyone else's. Dr. Turner got up and walked over to them.

"That large?" he whispered, sounding dazed.

"Yes. Carlos called it a meningioma. He was amazed at its degree of preservation. It's the slow-growing type that probably started in childhood. He's going to run a test to see if it was benign. The important thing to realize is that its growth would have caused abnormalities in her thought processes and behavior that grew worse with time."

"Oh, thank God, we have an answer, Ed!" Christine stood up to embrace her husband.

Gideon sent Heidi a glance that brought her to his side. He didn't have to say anything. The way he clutched her hand told her there was more.

Dr. Turner finally looked up at Gideon. Wiping his eyes, he said, "Did you find any trace of drugs?"

Gideon squeezed her fingers. "Morphine showed up in her bile, liver and urinary tract. It means she'd been on heroin and died of acute intoxication rather than smoke inhalation."

"Gideon!" Heidi squealed with joy. "Now we can go to Mr. Cobb and get the case reopened!" Forgetting everyone, she threw her arms around his neck.

"I know you're excited—so am I," he whispered into her hair. "The autopsy has helped us fill in numbers six and seven of our painting. But we're not home free yet. There are two more questions...."

The unexpected aside acted like a dash of ice water in her face. Slowly she let go of him. Looking up into his eyes, she said, "I don't understand."

He placed his hand on her shoulder, and she felt the tremor that passed through his body.

''For one thing,'' he said, ''we still have to find her supplier. Max is working on it right now.''

''But that might take a long time. Is it really necessary? Dr. Diaz will testify that she was on heroin.''

''We want this case airtight so we don't have to put Dana through another jury trial, don't we?''

''Yes, of course.'' She swallowed hard. ''What else?''

His eyes darkened in intensity.

She felt the first stirrings of panic. ''Tell me.''

''If there's someone out there who knew Amy planned to commit suicide, I want to find that person.''

''What if there isn't anyone?''

''Then the judge might say there's still reasonable doubt. At that point we'd have no choice but to take our chances with a new jury trial.''

''Obviously you don't think our chances are that good.''

He shook his head. ''You never know. It'll be hard to pick a jury that's not biased.''

Heidi bowed her head. ''If we've learned anything about Amy, it was that she was very shrewd. I'm not sure she would have trusted even Kristen or Stacy with that kind of secret.''

''Max'll scare the living daylights out of them if they don't come clean with what they know. All he has to do is tell them they could end up in prison for being accessories. It usually does the trick.

''At the very least they'll give him the name of the

person who sold Amy drugs. If we get lucky, they might let something else slip, as well."

"I think you'd better tell the Turners all this before they get too hopeful."

"Let's do it right now."

With the side of one finger, he removed the tears from her cheeks. She trembled at his touch, took a deep breath and turned around.

"Everybody? Gideon has a few more things to discuss. Why don't you all sit down and I'll bring in fresh coffee."

She needed to be alone for a moment to get her emotions under control. When she'd heard that Amy had been full of heroin, she'd assumed it was enough proof to get Dana out of prison.

That wasn't the case.

On her return from the kitchen with a fresh pot, her parents intercepted her. "I approve of him, Heidi," her dad murmured.

"Who wouldn't?" her mother chimed in, sounding emotional.

Heidi had known her folks would love him the minute they met him. She'd told them all about Kevin. If the boy ever gave them a chance, they'd love him, too.

"Gideon's incredible," she whispered as she refilled their cups.

"Here. Let me do the rest." Her mother took the pot from her. "You go back to him."

Heidi needed no urging. When she sat down next to Gideon, he slid his arm around her shoulders and pulled her close. "I was about to come and find you."

She curled up against him, then noticed that the Turners were more upset than she would have thought likely, even with the potential setback Gideon had described.

"What's wrong? Why are you both so unhappy?"

"Because we should have tried harder with Amy," Christine said between sobs. "I knew she wasn't... normal, but when Amy refused to go to Dr. Siricca for more sessions, I should've forced her to get help. We should've had tests done, just to see if there was anything abnormal. Why didn't we?" Her anguished cry rang throughout the living room.

"We made a lot of mistakes," Dr. Turner murmured with tears in his voice. "But I blame myself most of all for not agreeing to an autopsy when Mr. Cobb wanted it done."

His wife shook her head. "I couldn't bear the thought of it, either. It didn't seem necessary to do that to our little girl." She rocked back and forth in anguish. "I had no idea it could have helped Dana."

Dr. Turner shook his head as the tears rolled down his cheeks. "When I think how wrong we were! Our daughter's spent all this time in prison because of us." He stared at Heidi. "If it weren't for you... You've been the one to show us the way."

He swallowed. "We've talked it over with Gideon and have decided to ask Mr. Cobb to get a date for a hearing right away. By that time maybe we'll have the evidence Gideon is looking for—the proof that Amy intended to commit suicide. If not, we'll take our chances with a new jury trial."

Heidi turned to Gideon. "But I thought you wanted to go to the judge with an airtight case. If he calls for another jury, what if they come in with the same verdict as the old one?''

He caressed her arm through the silk blouse she was wearing. ''I'd like to believe that with all the new testimony, there's a sixty-forty chance they'll see those diary entries for what they really are.''

Heidi drew in her breath. ''But what if they don't?''

''Then we'll keep after that one vital piece of evidence until we find it. Even if it takes months. Or years.''

She remembered him saying those same words on the first night of class.

''I don't want it to take that long.''

Some emotion flickered in the depths of his eyes. ''Then let's get busy. We've got more work to do before we pick up Kevin. Why don't I follow you to your—'' His cell phone rang, interrupting him.

''Excuse me a moment. It's probably Max.''

After saying hello, he nodded to her, then got up from the couch to speak to his friend in private.

The conversation was over in seconds. When he put his phone back in his pocket, she saw the tension on his face and realized something vital had happened.

Anxious to hear, she rose to meet him. He took hold of her arm. ''I have to run down to headquarters to meet Max. Will you be here later?''

Don't you know I'll be wherever you want me to be? her heart cried. She was desperate to show him what he meant to her. But this wasn't the time.

''I'll stay to help clean up, then go back to the apartment.'' She fought not to let her disappointment show.

''Good. Just as long as I know where to find you.

Come with me while I say goodbye to the Turners and thank your parents, then walk me to the door. I need to be alone with you for a minute."

Between dark lashes, his eyes glinted with unmistakable desire. That look would have to sustain her while she waited for him to return.

ON THE WAY to headquarters, Gideon pulled out his cell phone. Judge Landers had jurisdiction over Dana's case. If Gideon wasn't mistaken, he and Daniel Mcfarlane were longtime golf buddies.

Since the Turners planned to contact Mr. Cobb immediately, Gideon wasn't above using every resource he had to get the case heard as soon as possible. He, too, was living for the day Dana walked out of prison a free woman.

By the time he'd parked underground, Daniel had agreed to get in touch with the judge. He assured Gideon he'd prevail upon Landers to act quickly.

Pleased by his response, Gideon was still smiling when he walked in the office and saw Max talking to Lieutenant Rodman. Their superior nodded to him.

"I hear you've all but pulled Jenke's case to pieces, and it's only day four! That's fast work, even for you, Poletti."

"I have my reasons."

The lieutenant shut the door of his inner office and darted Gideon a shrewd glance. "Like I said before, she must be some woman."

"Take it from me, she's a gorgeous redhead," Max interjected.

"A redhead? I guess that explains it," the lieutenant

quipped. "All right, you two. Bring me up-to-date. You go first, Poletti."

His boss listened without interrupting.

"...and since I was just told the results of the autopsy, I'm anxious to hear what Max learned when he talked to the girls."

The lieutenant's gaze switched to Max. "You haven't talked yet?"

Max shook his head. "When I phoned Gideon, he was at the Ellis home with the Turners. I told him to meet me at your office."

"Then let's hear what you've got."

"Yesterday Crandall set up surveillance on Kristen and Stacy, who live in a rented house with four other people, two of them guys. Our talks with the neighbors didn't give us the proof we needed, so we camped out to make sure we'd catch them before they went anywhere this morning.

"Kristen came out the front door first. We made our approach. After delivering a few home truths, I told her she and Stacy could talk to us inside or down at the station. They chose to cooperate.

"They got started on marijuana in high school. Now they're into the usual stuff you get with the campus crowd. Cocaine, ecstasy, you name it."

He pulled an envelope from his pocket and put it on the table. "The conversation's there on tape. I'm convinced neither of them had any idea Amy was planning suicide."

"Damn," Gideon muttered. "I was counting on one of them for that testimony."

"It doesn't mean Amy didn't tell someone else,"

Max said. "We'll just have to keep looking. But you're going to like the next part.

"The girls became friends with Amy when she enrolled in that alternative drama school. They were the ones who introduced her to marijuana. As time went on, she wanted more and got into LSD. About two months before she died, they said she complained of severe headaches and began snorting heroin because she had an aversion to needles."

"The tumor was responsible for the headaches. It all fits."

Max nodded. "The girls said she bought the expensive South American powder that comes in from the East Coast. The guy who sold it to her promised it was ninety-eight percent pure. Apparently he charged her a fortune for it."

"The autopsy showed acute morphine intoxication. That substantiates what the girls told you, because Carlos found no puncture wounds. Who's the supplier?"

Max looked at him. "A forty-two-year-old custodian at the drama school the girls used to attend. His name is Manny Fleischer. They only know him as Manny. Another student introduced them. Obviously he's found this a lucrative sideline.

"If that isn't interesting enough, remember the phone number you asked the department to track down? The one on the Turners' phone bills that weren't accounted for?"

Gideon nodded.

"It's Fleischer's cell-phone number. He lives in an expensive apartment in Sherman Heights. A custodian's salary alone wouldn't support that lifestyle.

Most of the students at that school have money—a constant source for ol' Manny. Like Amy, Kristen and Stacy come from affluent families. But they're so terrified of being linked with Amy's murder, they're willing to help us set up a sting.''

By now Gideon was on his feet. "How do they connect with him?"

"The routine is to call him early in the morning. He sets up the time they're supposed to come to the school. While students are shuffling between classes, the girls pass by his office and the transaction occurs."

"Let's move on it tomorrow!"

"I'm way ahead of you. The girls will be expecting us at their place early in the morning. As a precaution, I asked Crandall and Snow to tail them."

"Good. That leaves us free to focus on Fleischer."

"Well, gentlemen," their boss broke in, "it appears my presence is superfluous. Gideon? Congratulations on cracking this case so fast. I'd say you've got more than enough new evidence for her attorney to file a notice of hearing."

"Thanks, Lieutenant."

"How come you don't look happier about it?"

"The truth?"

"Always."

His hands formed fists. "I wanted Kristen or Stacy to testify that Amy planned to kill herself."

The lieutenant stood up. "I've been thinking about that. If she hoped to pin a murder rap on her sister, there's only one person she might have told—*if* she was desperate for a lethal dose of heroin."

Gideon stared at his boss. "Manny."

The older man nodded. "He'd be a safe bet. Drug dealers are like dead men. They don't tell tales."

"Unless they're faced with the prospect of life in prison," Max declared. "Come on, Gideon. We've got our work cut out."

He shook the lieutenant's hand. Gideon followed suit.

"How do I thank you for giving me this week?"

"Invite me to the wedding."

"There's nothing I'd like better."

"But?"

"Something tells me Heidi won't walk down the aisle with me unless Dana Turner's the maid of honor. She can't do that when she's locked up in Fielding Women's Prison."

"You mean to tell me your redhead isn't prepared to marry you this afternoon?"

He'd hit a nerve. "I don't know."

The older man squinted at him. "Shame on you, Poletti. For such a good detective, I'm surprised you haven't found the answer to that question yet."

"The boss has a point," Max said when they'd left the office and were making their way down to the underground garage.

"You know me. I like all my guns spiked first. However, it might interest you to know that after a conversation with Kevin at one-thirty this morning, I'm making progress in that direction."

"What happened?"

Gideon proceeded to tell him about the conversation. The comment concerning Frank provoked a volley of laughter from Max. Several cops turned in their direction.

"I swear it's all true. Before Kevin said good-night, he promised to be nice to Heidi."

"Good!"

"It's better than good, Max. He meant it."

"Then I don't see a problem."

"Once we've dealt with Manny Fleischer, maybe I'll agree with you."

"Follow me home so I can change clothes. If you're worried about Kevin with all this going on, he can sleep at our house tonight. I'll ask Gabriella to leave work early and pick him up after school. She'll love the company."

"If it won't put her out, that would be terrific. I'll phone Heidi and tell her about the change in plans. Maybe she's still with her folks."

Gideon's heart kicked into high gear at the thought of hearing her voice.

CHAPTER FIFTEEN

HEIDI HAD JUST FINISHED putting the silverware in the buffet drawer when her cell phone rang. It was Gideon! She was so excited about seeing him again, she felt almost sick to her stomach.

"Hello, Gideon," she said after the first ring. "Where are you?"

"I was about to ask you the same question."

"I'm still at Mom's. Can you come over here, or do you want us to meet at my apartment? What would be easiest for you?"

The slight hesitation on his part immediate dampened her spirits. "Max and I have business that's going to take us well into tomorrow or even the next day. I may have to cancel class."

Her hand tightened on the phone. *Don't you dare let your disappointment show, Heidi Ellis.*

"Does this have to do with Kristen and Stacy?"

"Yes. I'll tell you all about it when I see you."

He was being too mysterious. "Please don't do anything dangerous," she said anxiously.

"What we'll be working on is strictly routine."

Gideon was a pro at downplaying everything. "I'm beginning to understand Kevin's fears. Loving someone who fixes computers or works on teeth is quite a different proposition from loving a man whose career is in law enforcement.''

"Heidi..." His voice was so deep and husky she hardly recognized it.

"I love you so much, Gideon, you can't imagine."

"Do you have any idea how long I waited to hear those words?" he asked. "What a hell of a time you've picked to tell me!"

"I didn't pick it," she said. "The words just came out."

"Thank God," he whispered. "I think you know I fell in love with you the first night we met."

A sob caught in her throat. "I hoped...even before I knew whether you were free."

"I'm not free *now*," he asserted with the bold honesty that was such an innate part of him. "You've got me snagged so hard and tight you'll never be rid of me."

"Do you think I'd ever let you go?"

"You don't mind that I come with a fourteen-year-old son?"

"Mind? Gideon! You're talking to an only child who always wanted a full house! I'm sure it's what drove me to become a teacher. Make no mistake—I fell in love with you *and* Kevin. He's part of you. You're both wonderful!

"Will you let me pick him up after school, Gideon? I'll take him to your house and spend both nights with him, if necessary. We need time to learn we can be friends. It'll work, because our common denominator is *you*."

For a moment there was silence. "Heidi?"

"What?"

"Please tell me I'm not dreaming this conversation."

"You're not," came her tremulous response. "I'll be outside his school at three o'clock, exactly the way we were yesterday. As soon as I've hustled him into my car, we'll call you to prove that everyone's very much awake—not dreaming at all—and waiting for you to come home."

His voice sounded ragged as he said, "After all these years of wondering if my ideal woman would ever materialize, you couldn't possibly know how good that sounds to me. I love you, Heidi Ellis."

"And I love you, Gideon. Take care."

She turned off the phone and ran in her stocking feet to the living room, where her parents were talking.

"Guess what?"

They both broke into laughter.

"What?" Heidi smiled.

Her father shook his head. "Oh, honey. We know."

"We've known for several weeks," her mother added.

"I'm so happy I feel like I'm going to burst. You've got to meet Kevin! While Gideon's winding up Dana's case, I'll be taking care of his son for a few days."

"Bring him over. We'll go fishing."

"I'm sure he'd love that! Uh-oh, it's already ten after two. Where are my shoes? I've got to get going. I'll see you later. Thank you for everything. I could tell Gideon was crazy about you."

"We're crazy about him for putting the light back

in your eyes. There was a time we wondered if we'd see it again.''

"I didn't know a man like him existed. He's... selfless.''

"The Turners said the same about you, honey. Of course, your mother and I already knew that about you. I'd say you and Gideon are both very lucky to have found each other.''

Her father's words stayed with her all the way to Kevin's school. She arrived with ten minutes to spare. Two school buses were lined up in front. She parked behind them, but the euphoria she'd been feeling earlier had worn off. Nervousness had replaced it.

It was one thing to *sound* confident when she'd told Gideon she'd take care of Kevin. But it was quite another to *be* confident when he was about to come out and find his father's girlfriend waiting for him.

If worse came to worst, he'd ask her to drive him to his mother's place of work. Heidi was prepared for that, but she hoped against hope he'd give her a chance.

Once the bell rang, the school started to empty. She got out of the car and went over to the flagpole, where she'd be sure to see him. Several minutes passed before she saw him, walking with another boy, who looked familiar. It had to be Brad, his friend who'd had the birthday party.

When they were close enough that she didn't have to shout, she called to him. Both heads turned in her direction.

"Hi!" Kevin seemed surprised, but she didn't see any hostility in his eyes. "Where's Dad?"

"He's working. I offered to pick you up. Do you mind?"

He adjusted his backpack. "No."

On a stroke of inspiration she said, "How about your friend? Brad, isn't it? Would you like a ride? I'd be happy to drive you."

"That's okay. I was planning to take the bus."

"Come on," Kevin urged him.

"Maybe you'd like to come home with us. I have a cell phone. You could call your mom and see if it's all right. Tell her we're going out for pizza and hot-fudge sundaes first."

"Do it!" Kevin's enthusiasm encouraged her as nothing else could have. The boys had a brief powwow. She heard Brad say something about Kevin's mom never letting his friends stay for dinner on a school night. There was more whispering.

Finally Kevin said, "He's going to come with us. Let's go!" They ran to her car and were already inside before she could even slide behind the wheel.

"Here." She handed Kevin her cell phone. "Your dad wants you to call him. Why don't you do that first, then Brad can phone home?"

"Okay. Thanks."

Soon she could hear him talking to Gideon. He sounded happy, animated, the way a healthy young man should. After a couple of minutes he handed her the phone. "Dad wants to talk to you."

There were more hushed whispers in the back seat as she put the phone to her ear.

"Gideon?"

"So far so good?" he asked.

"Yes."

"I told him I might not be home for a couple of days, and that you'd offered to stay with him. He took the news very well, indeed."

"I'm so relieved. What if I ask Brad to sleep over tonight?"

"Are you willing to do that?"

"I think it might make Kevin feel more comfortable, considering it's his first night alone with me."

"Your instincts are obviously reliable. Sure, go ahead. I just wish I could join your slumber party. I can guarantee *you* wouldn't get any sleep."

"Gideon!" Heat crept over her face.

"That's what happens when two people who are madly in love go on their honeymoon. I did understand you right, didn't I? You *are* going to marry me, aren't you?"

She couldn't believe he was proposing to her while the boys were hanging on her every word.

"Yes!" To her embarrassment, it sounded more like a squeak than a word.

He let out a delighted chuckle. "Fine. We'll talk about wedding plans the next time I hold you in my arms. If I'm moving too fast for you, I refuse to apologize."

"I don't want you to apologize. I want what you want. As soon as possible."

"You do choose your moments, don't you, Heidi? Let me warn you, so do I."

The line went dead.

GIDEON MARVELED that he could be at the jail at any time of the day or night and the place teemed with life, but never more so than on Saturday mornings. It was a holding tank for arrestees like Manny Fleischer, who often became violent, so it was a particularly ugly underworld.

He'd made a call to John Cobb at five-thirty that morning. The attorney had said he'd meet him there at seven. Gideon sat in a chair with his head against the wall, trying to catch a little sleep while he waited.

Yesterday afternoon with the help of the girls, he and Max had been able to make a successful arrest at the school. But it had taken until this morning for the smarmy custodian to agree to talk.

Gideon had sent Max home to Gaby hours ago. The thought of home held a brand-new meaning for Gideon. Heidi had left a message on his voice mail saying that she and Kevin had spent Friday night at her parents and were planning to go fishing today.

Though it thrilled him that the relationship between Heidi and his son was going so well, he couldn't wait to be alone with her again. There was so much to tell her he hardly knew where to begin.

"Detective Poletti?"

He opened bleary eyes to discover the well-known criminal attorney standing a few feet away. Impeccably shaved and dressed in a suit, the man's appearance reminded Gideon he hadn't had a shower or shave in two days.

"Mr. Cobb." He rose to his feet and the two men shook hands. "I'm sorry to have woken you so early. Thanks for coming down here."

"Call me John and don't apologize. Ever since Heidi

Ellis phoned and told me she was determined to get Dana's case reopened, I've been eager to meet with you.

"In my career I've only lost two cases where I knew in my gut the person was innocent. Dana Turner's one of them."

Gideon nodded. "I felt the same thing during my first visit with her at the prison."

"Her parents came to my office on Thursday afternoon," John said. "Because of the evidence you've uncovered, I had my paralegal prepare notices of hearing. Before the day was out, a courier delivered them to Ron Jenke and Judge Landers.

"To my surprise I received a call from the judge yesterday afternoon. He's cleared his calendar to hear the case on Tuesday."

Three days from now. *Thank you, Daniel.*

"It's unprecedented and has put Ron in a tailspin," John continued. "But he isn't fighting it, because even he understands that the results of the autopsy have changed the entire case.

"He knows we're armed with a lot more ammunition that challenges the jury's finding on the circumstantial evidence." He shook his head. "Still, it's a damn shame the Turners wouldn't permit an autopsy the first time around."

"I agree."

"After we finish here, I need you in my office. My staff has agreed to work overtime. We've got a case to prepare. I've instructed my secretary to clear my calendar through Tuesday so we can work nonstop."

"I'll dash home to clean up, then join you." Gideon's reunion with Heidi and Kevin would have to wait a little longer.

"Good."

"John, Kristen and Stacy are willing to testify that Amy talked about her hatred of Dana on many occasions. But there's one piece of evidence missing."

"You mean testimony that Amy planned to kill herself?" The other man nodded. "I'm well aware of that. Let's go and see what we can get out of Mr. Fleischer."

WATCHING A FEMALE police officer escort a handcuffed Dana into the courtroom made Heidi thankful she hadn't had to witness the painful sight the first time. She was overwhelmed by the indignity of Dana's treatment, the humiliations.

How had her friend stood the horror of it?

Swallowing a sob, Heidi, who sat between both sets of parents, clung to the hands of her mother and Christine.

All eyes were focused on Dana, whose pallor gave a translucent quality to her lovely face. She was wearing a skirt and blouse Heidi recognized, but the clothes hung on her thin body.

She moved gracefully as she took her place at the table, where Mr. Cobb sat with Gideon and Dr. Diaz. The other witnesses who'd been called in to testify, among them Kristen and Stacy, sat in the row behind them.

Max and Gaby sat a few seats away with Kevin. Unbeknownst to Heidi until a half hour ago, he'd begged his father to get him excused from school so he could watch the proceedings.

Because Gideon had been forced to work with Mr. Cobb all weekend, Heidi had ended up spending Sunday with the boy. In those three days she felt he'd learned to trust her. They were comfortable around each other now. He made a little motion with his hand when their gazes met. The gesture warmed her heart. She waved back.

On the other side of the room sat Mr. Jenke with his legal team. He appeared innocuous, but she'd learned enough about him to know he could be a pit bull in court.

There were other people assembled that Heidi didn't recognize. Probably friends or relatives of the witnesses. According to Gideon, the man who'd sold Amy drugs was being held under guard outside the doors and wouldn't make an appearance until it was his turn to testify.

While she looked from Dana to Gideon, Heidi had to wipe her eyes. A month ago she'd been at an all-time low over her friend and hadn't even heard of Detective Gideon Poletti.

So much about her world had changed since then. She was in love.

Please, God, let Dana's world change, too. Allow her the opportunity to come home and be a comfort to her family. Allow her to move about freely again...to fall in love...

"All rise."

The judge entered the courtroom. Heidi stared at the man with the steel-rimmed glasses. He would decide

Dana's fate. He alone had the power to order a new trial by jury or set her free.

Let him be a wise, discerning judge...

"The court of the Honorable Quinton T. Landers is now in session. You may be seated."

THROUGHOUT THE HEARING, tremendous tension had been building. Gideon watched Ron Jenke get up to cross-examine Kristen. According to John, she'd be the last one to testify before Fleischer took the stand. After the summations by the attorneys, it was up to the judge. Gideon's breathing felt constricted.

"Ms. Welch, in the trial last August, you testified that Amy Turner was terrified her sister, Dana, was going to kill her."

"That's what she told me."

"Yet just now you testified to the court that you knew Amy Turner hated her sister with a violent passion. Furthermore you admitted that you and Stacy and Amy were all heavy drug users. Why did you withhold that information at the first trial?"

Kristen hunched her shoulders. "Because you never asked me those questions. Before it started, you told me just to answer what I had to and not volunteer anything."

Her simple, truthful response had to be devastating to Ron Jenke. Gideon exchanged a meaningful glance with John.

"I have no more questions of this witness, your Honor."

The judge told Kristen to step down. "Mr. Cobb? Do you have any more witnesses?"

"One more, Your Honor."

"Go ahead."

"I'd like to call Mr. Manny Fleischer to the stand. If the sergeant-at-arms would escort him in."

Subdued for the moment, the slight, benign-looking man entered from a side door, handcuffed and closely guarded. The lowlife had been pushing drugs on teens for years. He deserved to be sentenced to life! But John had worked out a plea bargain with him if he'd testify. Now it was in the judge's hands. Considering that Dana's release hung in the balance, though, it was worth it.

After Fleischer was sworn in, John Cobb got up from the table.

"State your name for the court."

"Manny Fleischer."

"Your age?"

"Forty-two," he muttered.

"You'll have to speak up, Mr. Fleischer," the judge warned him.

"Forty-two!"

"Your address?"

"3010 Windward Drive, Sherman Heights."

"What do you do for a living, Mr. Fleischer?"

"I'm a custodian."

"Where?"

"Pickford Alternative Drama High School."

"How long have you been employed there?"

"I don't know… Ten years."

Gideon shook his head. That was too long for him to get away with corrupting kids.

"Would you please tell the court the reason for your arrest Friday afternoon?"

He rolled his eyes. "I got caught selling ecstasy to some students."

"In fact, we've just heard from two of those students, who took the witness stand a few minutes ago. Do you see them in the courtroom?"

The man nodded.

"The court needs a spoken answer, Mr. Fleischer."

"Yes!"

"Did you ever sell drugs to Amy Turner?"

"Yes!"

"What kind of drugs?"

"Ecstasy, smack, death wish, LSD."

"We've heard testimony that a few months before she died, she starting buying heroin. Is that true?"

"Yes! I already told you—smack."

"Both Kristen and Stacy have testified that on the day Amy died, they drove to the school so she could buy more heroin from you. Is that true?"

"Yes!"

"Why do you think she changed to heroin?"

He hunched his shoulders. "She wanted a bigger buzz."

"In order to live at that address in Sherman Heights, you would have to charge a lot for the stuff you sell."

"Like a lot of the kids, she was good for it."

"Except that she didn't have any money on the day she died. So how come she went home with a larger amount of heroin than usual? What kind of negotiations were worked out?"

"She gave me her ATM card and the pin number.

She said I could withdraw the money as soon as she deposited her tuition check. I knew her dad had the bucks, so I figured why not.''

Gideon closed his eyes. He knew where John was going with this. The man was brilliant. *Just keep it up...*

''How much did you give her?''

''A lot.''

''Because you wanted the money.''

''Sure.''

''Was it enough to kill her?''

''If she snorted it all in one go.''

''Do you think that's what she intended?''

''I'm no mind reader. All she told me was that she was going to take the trip of trips.''

A jolt rocked Gideon's body. *That was it! That was the testimony he'd been waiting for!*

''Thank you, Mr. Fleischer. I have no more questions.''

The judge turned to Ron Jenke.

''You wish to cross-examine?''

''No, Your Honor.''

''You may step down, Mr. Fleischer.''

As the drug pusher was escorted out of the courtroom, Ron Jenke said, ''If it would please the court, I would like to make a statement at this time and forgo my final summation.''

''Is that all right with you, Mr. Cobb?''

''Yes, Your Honor.''

''Go ahead, Mr. Jenke.''

He rose slowly to his feet, but didn't move from behind the table. ''Considering the evidence presented, it's clear to me that Amy Turner planned her own death to create the impression that her sister murdered her. It is my belief that a gross miscarriage of justice has been done to Dana Turner.''

He turned to took at the woman seated next to Gideon. ''I apologize to you, Ms. Turner, and to your family, for the pain you've been forced to endure.

''Your Honor—'' he addressed the judge once more ''—I'd like to make the motion that this young woman go free.''

There were cries of joy in the courtroom, among them, Heidi's. Gideon couldn't refrain from covering one of Dana's freezing hands with his own. She didn't move. She was still in shock.

The judge took off his glasses and leaned forward. ''Thank you, Mr. Jenke, for your gracious apology to the Turner family and the court. Our system isn't perfect, but it does allow for grievances to be revisited and, as in this case, rectified.

''I concur with both counselors that Amy Turner took her own life. Therefore, I vacate my former decision. Dana Turner, as of this moment you're a free woman. Please remove her handcuffs.''

The female police officer quietly did his bidding.

''There. I'm sure that feels better.'' The judge spoke directly to Dana with a compassionate smile. ''It is the hope of this court that in time you can put the worst of this experience behind you.

''So much of my work deals with the ugly. Today we've all witnessed something beautiful. For that, I would like to commend the fine investigative work of

Detective Gideon Poletti. You're an honor to the badge you carry.''

He gazed out at the audience. ''Court is adjourned.'' After pounding the gavel, he left the podium.

The sound seemed to bring Dana to life. She turned to Gideon. The next thing he knew he was being hugged by a woman whose happy sobs resonated in his soul.

WHILE HER PARENTS and the Turners dashed down to the front of the courtroom, Heidi hung back for a moment, savoring the sight of the man she loved embracing her dearest friend.

''Heidi?''

''Kevin!'' She grabbed Gideon's son and rocked him in a hug, so full of happiness she couldn't contain it. ''Your father did it! He's so wonderful! I love him so much!''

The boy lifted a beaming face to her. ''He's the greatest.''

''He is. Let's go get him.''

On their way down to the front, she hugged Max and Gaby, then introduced Kevin to John Cobb and the various witnesses whose testimony had helped turn everything around.

Suddenly she heard her name being called. Dana was running toward her. They met halfway and threw their arms around each other. While the tears ran nonstop, neither of them could find words. Soon both sets of parents had joined them in a group embrace.

''Do you think there's room in there for one more?'' asked a familiar male voice.

Heidi caught sight of Gideon's brilliant blue eyes. "Darling!" She launched herself at him. A pair of powerful arms caught her. He crushed her against his body, and she clung to him, trying to tell him, trying to show him how she felt.

"Let's get out of here," he whispered against her lips. "We have plans to make."

She lifted shining eyes to him. "Gaby told me she and Max drove to Las Vegas to get married. Why don't we do the same?"

"When?"

"Right now. We can be back tomorrow. The Calders said they'd watch Kevin overnight."

His body stilled. "What about your parents?"

"I'm not marrying them."

"No. You're not." His handsome face broke out in a smile.

"When we get back, we'll plan a big church wedding with all our friends and family. But I don't want to wait another second to be your wife."

"My fantasy really is coming true."

"I hope it includes children, because Kevin and I had a heart-to-heart while you were gone."

"Is that so?"

"Yes. When I told him I'd always wanted a little brother or sister, he said he'd always wished for one, too."

Gideon's eyes ignited.

"He said his mom was through having kids, but he knew you wanted more. I'm pretty sure it was Kevin's way of telling me it was all right if we got married."

His hands grasped her arms and caressed them. "The

news keeps getting better and better. The truth is, I want you pregnant with my child as soon as I can make it happen.'' His voice shook as he said the words.

''You don't want that as much as I do. There's just one problem. I'm not sure Kevin's ready for us to go away on a honeymoon.''

''I know he's not, but just living with you will feel like we're on one.''

''Well,'' she whispered, ''get ready to be loved like you've never been loved before. There may be days I'll lock you in our bedroom so you can't leave me.''

''Heidi…'' His eyes glistened.

''It's true. While I was listening to the judge's final remarks, I realized how precious life is. There's not a moment to waste.

''Unless you want me to work, I'm not planning to teach in the fall. Pregnant or not, I'm going to make a home for you and Kevin. I'm prepared to indulge my private detective for as long as he wants.''

She pressed her mouth to his, offering him a taste of the glories that awaited them.

ON FRIDAY EVENING Gideon handed a prize to Bob, the student who scored highest on the test given after the coroner's visit. The pocket dictionary of police and legal terms was another instant hit.

When the noise subsided, he said, ''If you recall, Heidi read us a synopsis about a woman wasting away in prison. This woman had been wrongfully accused of murdering her sister. At the time she didn't know the story's ending.''

Everyone nodded and made comments about what an emotional story it was.

"I have it on good authority that she's finished it now. Heidi? I hope you don't mind my springing this on you, but I'm sure the rest of the class would like to hear how it all turned out."

His wife of three heavenly days and nights shot him a surprised glance before getting to her feet. He watched the way her shimmering red-gold hair swung about her shoulders. A memory as recent as two hours ago assailed him—of burying his face in that glorious hair after they'd made love.

"Well, this is the way I ended the story. The woman named Dana had a friend who believed in her innocence. By some miracle, this friend, a teacher, learned that a homicide detective was teaching a night class on criminology in her room.

"So she joined his class to see if she could learn how to conduct a criminal investigation herself. Instead, she fell headlong in love with the handsome detective and his son."

Everyone started smiling. Gideon should have guessed his wife would pull something like this for putting her on the spot. But he didn't mind. He was so crazy about her, he couldn't think straight.

"Out of the goodness of his heart, he told her he'd investigate the case if she'd act as his assistant. In less than a week he turned the whole case around, and Dana Turner is now a free woman," she said with tears in her voice.

"It seems her sister, Amy, suffered from a brain tumor that twisted her mind and led her to take drugs.

In the end she committed suicide, but arranged it to look as though her sister had murdered her.

"This detective had suspected drugs all along. He insisted an autopsy be performed that hadn't been done at the time of the death because the family couldn't bear to have their daughter's body violated. That's how they felt about it, but he convinced them it needed to be done to get at the truth.

"He asked the best coroner in the county to do the job. Dr. Carlos Diaz. The report stated that a tumor was found, along with traces of morphine in the liver. It proved the victim died from an overdose of heroine, not carbon monoxide poisoning as the initial medical report had revealed."

Emily's hand shot up. "You're talking about you and Detective Poletti."

"Yes!" Nancy blurted.

"I knew it!"

"We all knew it!" Carol shouted.

Heidi looked at him with adoring eyes. "It terrifies me to think what would have happened if he hadn't agreed to teach this class for Daniel Mcfarlane.

"Because we met, my friend is free to pursue her life, and I found the man of my dreams. Just so you know, my last name is Poletti now. Gideon and I were married on Tuesday night. That's why he had to cancel Wednesday's class.

"Kevin would be here, but he decided he'd rather go fishing with my dad, his new grandpa."

Everyone burst into applause, then they all jumped out of their chairs to hug both Heidi and Gideon and give their congratulations. Amid the excited tumult, Heidi's gaze met his.

"I love you." She mouthed the words he couldn't hear often enough.

As Gideon mouthed the same words back, he knew life didn't get any better than this.

When class was over, he intended to drive her to Daniel's house. It was time to show her off and thank his mentor for the opportunity that had brought him his soul mate.

He could already hear what Daniel would say...

"I knew you didn't *really* want to take that class over for me. You thought it'd be a big bore. That'll teach you to remember my number-one rule—never assume anything."

A heartwarming new series by
Carolyn McSparren

Creature Comfort, the largest veterinary clinic in Tennessee, treats animals of all sizes—horses and cattle as well as family pets. Meet the patients—and their owners. And share the laughter and the tears with the men and women who love and care for all creatures great and small.

#996 THE MONEY MAN
(July 2001)

#1011 THE PAYBACK MAN
(September 2001)

Look for these Harlequin Superromance titles coming soon to your favorite retail outlet.

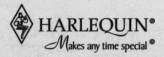

COMING SOON...

AN EXCITING
OPPORTUNITY TO SAVE
ON THE PURCHASE OF
HARLEQUIN AND
SILHOUETTE BOOKS!

*DETAILS TO FOLLOW
IN OCTOBER 2001!*

YOU WON'T WANT TO MISS IT!

PHQ401

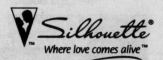

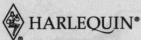

Harlequin truly does make any time special. ... This year we are celebrating weddings in style!

A Walk Down the Aisle
WEDDING CELEBRATION

To help us celebrate, we want you to tell us how wearing the Harlequin wedding gown will make your wedding day special. As the grand prize, Harlequin will offer one lucky bride the chance to **"Walk Down the Aisle" in the Harlequin wedding gown!**

There's more...

For her honeymoon, she and her groom will spend five nights at the **Hyatt Regency Maui.** As part of this five-night honeymoon at the hotel renowned for its romantic attractions, the couple will enjoy a candlelit dinner for two in Swan Court, a sunset sail on the hotel's catamaran, and duet spa treatments.

Maui • Molokai • Lanai

To enter, please write, in, 250 words or less, how wearing the Harlequin wedding gown will make your wedding day special. The entry will be judged based on its emotionally compelling nature, its originality and creativity, and its sincerity. This contest is open to Canadian and U.S. residents only and to those who are 18 years of age and older. There is no purchase necessary to enter. Void where prohibited. See further contest rules attached. Please send your entry to:

Walk Down the Aisle Contest

In Canada	In U.S.A.
P.O. Box 637	P.O. Box 9076
Fort Erie, Ontario	3010 Walden Ave.
L2A 5X3	Buffalo, NY 14269-9076

You can also enter by visiting www.eHarlequin.com
Win the Harlequin wedding gown and the vacation of a lifetime!
The deadline for entries is October 1, 2001.

HARLEQUIN®
Makes any time special ®

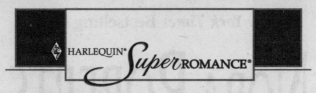